Claimed by the Savage Alien Orxlon

Supernova Escapes

EDEN EMBER
STARR HUNTRESS

Cover by Starr Huntress / Partial Image
Credit: Deposit Photos.com
Edited by Perfectly Plotted Books
ISBN: 9798598881934
Imprint: Independently published

Chapter 1

RAVEN

Flames rushed by the window as we entered Mor's atmosphere. Entering Earth's atmosphere didn't cause as much of a burn. The flames lapped at the windows and heat poured from the thick glass to the point that I feared my hair might singe. It was too late to back out now. My white-knuckled fist lifted to fan the warmth from my face as the *Starden Express* careened toward Mor's dusty surface. I questioned why I took the vacation as my life flashed before my eyes.

The Kornian brushed purple hair from her larger-than-life eyes as she smiled at me. "Congratulations. After taking your vitals and blood, we've found the perfect planet, in a star system far from here where you can breathe the atmosphere and enjoy the luxury vacation of your dreams," Staklo said. Her eyes blinked separately, reminding me of a chameleon back on Earth.

I had a hard time deciding whether she was looking at me or looking at something else to one side of me or the other. Being the only other person in the room, I assumed I was her focus. "I'm very excited about it," I replied. I entered the contest for the *Starlight Dream Vacation* through the *Supernova Escapes Agency* three months ago. I had given up on being selected just before

Staklo called to congratulate me on being chosen for the vacation.

The lone one on the trip, I gathered my wits after the rough landing and unbuckled the straps holding me in place. The giant plume of dust caused by the ship landing soon began to coat the hangar as we waited until it dissipated to open the hatch. The natives of Mor wore protective face coverings to keep the dust out of their faces. The long red scarf I brought to wear with my cocktail dress worked perfectly as a face covering for me. I didn't care that my pink and beige outfit didn't match it at all.

"Your transport ship will arrive shortly. Have a seat and get some food from the bar if you are hungry," Talia, the female Barxicon, told me. Her long eyelashes fluttered a bit as she smiled. She looked something like a caricature of a human, with a ridiculously enormous face and eyes made up like a cosmetics model. I bit my tongue to keep from laughing at her.

Talia disappeared. I nibbled on a small bowl of fruit, which looked and tasted like miniature cherries. Mor held little attraction for me other than the fact that it's not Earth. For me, it was just a stopover where I would wait for my ride to the ultimate vacation destination. Astavail sounded so dreamy as I read about it. According to the brochure, it had lush green herbaceous plants and trees, as well as deep indigo waters, which were claimed to be perfectly safe for humans to swim in. This was why I packed two swimsuits, one of which I paid over nine hundred dollars for when it was on sale. The other one, a white crocheted number, would look great against my tanned skin, if I ever reached the paradise planet.

"Finally." I plucked out the makeup mirror to adjust my lip color. The *Remis* landed safely, causing a giant dust plume to rain over the hangar. I waited for the dust to settle before I stepped out with my bags in tow. It was a gigantic ship for a transport ship. So big, in fact, it took up most of the airfield.

I waited at the gate, watching with bated breath as the hatch slowly opened. Little creatures scurried off, paying no attention to me. The bronzed god appeared and his golden eyes settled upon me as he approached. My breath caught for a moment, as his hair flowed back long and wild, as if he'd ridden a motorcycle across the desert. Muscles were built upon muscles, and I had to stop staring as he advanced. A small smile formed on his full lips as he stared a hole through me. I had to double check to make certain that no part of my chest was showing because of the way he stared at me.

"Well?" his voice boomed.

I jumped, not expecting such a deep tone. "Well, what?" I asked.

"Are you ready to go? The *Remis* doesn't stay planetside for very long. Not on Mor, anyway. Come, we go now," he said to me as he pivoted.

The little creatures, which reminded me of garden gnomes, scurried up the hatch while carrying crates from the hangar. "Aerk, Dron, pick up the pace," the savage alien boomed. The creatures let out a wail as their little legs moved faster and they took off in a run.

"You, come on. Time to go," he barked.

"What? I don't know who you are or what you think you're doing by ordering me around. I'm not one of your crewmembers," I spat as I cowered back from the hulking beast.

He advanced toward me, his thick brow knit together sharply. "I came to this dust pit to pick up a Raven Madela, a Terran from Earth. Are you not this Raven?"

"I am. But who the hell are you?" I asked. No one at the Supernova Escapes Agency warned me about the savage alien running the transport ship.

He straightened, towering over me. "I am Orxlon, a Salzonian from Salzoni in the Humbaba System. I own the *Remis*. You are to come with me."

"I'm supposed to go to Astavail. I won a Starlight Dream Vacation." I straightened my own stance and lifted my chin, showing the animal how he didn't scare me in the least.

The wind picked up and plumes of dust lifted and fell. In the distance, a dark foreboding cloud swirled. Orxlon jerked his head in that direction.

"We need to go. Get on the ship," he barked.

"No, I think I'll stay here and wait for the next transport--"

He didn't listen as he lurched forward, grabbing me and lifting me up. Dust swirled as the wind pelted us.

"No! Put me down, you beast!" I screamed. No one came from the interior of the hangar to rescue me. Orxlon nodded toward my bags and the little grunts that scurried nearby did his bidding. My fists beat on his back as he walked up the ramp onto the *Remis*. "Put me down!"

Once onboard the great ship, the hatch closed and only then did the brute set me down. My hands slid over his massive muscles as he glared down at me. "Stop fighting. The dust storm is terrible. Lift off is imminent, or else this dirt rock is our home for weeks," Orxlon warned.

I blinked up at him. My body reacted in a strange way to his sexy stance, those muscles, and his direct manner. But the feminist part of me bucked at being treated like some little thing to be handled. My hands quickly found my hips. "I do not appreciate the manner with which you handled me," I declared.

He snorted. "Better get used to it," Orxlon said as he stepped away. Before he got too far, he turned back to glare at me. "Well, you had better follow me so that we can lift off before the storm hits. Unless you like it rough and enjoy being slammed against the walls?" His brow lifted.

"What? No! Let me off this prison," I spat.

"Okay, have it your way," he replied. The muscular being strode toward me, and instead of opening the hatch, grabbed me again and threw me over his shoulder.

"What the--" I beat my hands uselessly on his back. "Put me down, you brute!"

He chuckled, the deep reverberation resounding throughout his chest and back as he marched ahead as if I weighed nothing. We trailed through the ship until he came to a room and set me down hard in a chair. "Buckle up, we're leaving immediately."

I stared at him while frozen in my spot. The little crewmembers dumped my bags just inside the doorway. He stared at me and motioned toward the belt on the seat. I didn't budge. "Suit yourself. When the ship takes off, you'll be thrown around." He strode out of the room, the door closing by the time I had hopped up and rushed toward it.

"Dammit!" I pounded on the locked door, but no one came to my rescue. Looking around the room, I found nothing to help me open the door except for a bunk bed built into the wall, a chair with straps, and a water closet. Other than that, the dark gray walls and dim lighting did little for the appeal of the place. Suddenly, an alarm blared. I adjusted my ear implant to understand the gargle of words.

"Flight in sixty seconds," came the voice.

Fresh hot tears stained my eyes as I had no choice but to sit in the chair and tighten the straps around my body. I realized my bags were loose, so I quickly unstrapped and shoved the bags under the bunk bed, inside the storage compartments. The great ship vibrated as I dove for the chair. I had to grab hold as the place shuddered during lift-off. The straps barely tightened around me when the ship took an upward stance, nosing up through the atmosphere of Mor. I had no windows, so I couldn't tell exactly what was happening. My fists beat my thighs.

"Damn you, Orxlon. You will pay for this!"

The straps fell away as I stood soon after the ship's motion calmed. The door remained locked, yet I beat on it anyway. "Please, Orxlon, let me out! If the ship is in flight, I can't escape," I yelled.

No one came, and my stomach began to growl from hunger. "Hey, I would like something to eat." Though I tried to listen at the door, I couldn't hear what was happening outside in the corridor. It felt like hours had passed since he had so rudely carried me onto the ship. Despite my angst, I crawled onto the bunk and settled on my back, looking up at the compartments just above. Odd formations in the white metal stared back at me. My finger traced them until I rolled to my side and my eyes shut. The door opening later startled me as I quickly sat up and banged my head on the edge of the upper compartments over the bed.

"Oh, I see you've made yourself comfortable," Orxlon said as he walked into the room, the door closing behind him.

"Yes, well, out of boredom," I complained.

"Come join me in the dining room," he told me as he headed back toward the door. It wasn't a question, but a demand. When I didn't jump at his words, he turned back to look at me. "Unless you want to go all night without food?"

I reluctantly rose from the bed and followed him out of the room. His long legs strode ahead and I had to run to keep up. "Are you going to keep me locked up the entire time?" I asked.

He snorted. "Only if necessary. I can't have an angry Terran loose on this ship. You misbehaved earlier and I have to maintain order on my ship," he reasoned.

"I wasn't misbehaving. You took me against my will. I wanted to stay on Mor," I replied.

"And I came all this way to carry you to Astavail." His expression caused me to step back.

"I'm sorry, but I don't take kindly to your use of force on me. Perhaps had you shown a little kindness, I might have reacted differently."

We turned through a door to the dining room. Food was arrayed over the large thick table and it made my mouth water. I took a seat while he sat down across from me, his stern face set on mine. "Kindness? I *am* being kind. Perhaps you don't know about Salzonians. We aren't like weak Terrans. Our royal race embodies strength and power," he informed me.

"And a good dose of rudeness," I replied.

"You would do well to realize how much out of my way I went to fetch you from that place," he answered.

"And you would do well to turn this ship around and take me back to Mor," I retorted as I filled my plate with the alien food.

"What do you plan to do there?"

"Ask for a prompt refund for this vacation from hell," I said with a smirk.

"You *won* the vacation. You can't receive a refund for something that you won."

"Then, I just want to go back to Earth. Supernova Escapes can have their lousy paradise vacation," I spat back.

"Yes, let's go back to Mor." He left me in the dining hall to finish my food with the satisfaction of my request. I would get what I wanted after Orxlon treated me so terribly.

Chapter 2

I'd show her. Mor was uninhabitable, and she'd see with her own eyes just how dreadful it would be to land there. Supernova Escapes Agency delivered on their promise of finding the perfect mate for me. They should, I paid with the worth of the crown jewels of my planet for their one hundred percent guarantee of a perfect match. The moment I laid eyes upon Raven, the shift in my chest surprised me. That's how much I knew she would be mine. She just hadn't realized it yet. Peering down at my chest, it pounded outward, three hearts in unison. Never had that happened before now. Raven would be mine. My mind no longer played a role in my urges. My hearts compelled me far more than any intellect could.

Raven's resistance to me would prove a problem. I didn't think that I'd have such a difficult task in convincing the beautiful creature to let me claim her. Instead, she's resisted me from the very beginning. Perhaps she didn't see my status as the owner of the ship and a flock of servants at my command as suitable for her. In time, I'd change her mind, coax her, force her if need be. I'm not accustomed to being denied what I want.

"You have freedom to walk about as you wish," I said

"

to her.

Raven regarded me as she sat in a lump on the strapped chair in her room. "When will we make it back to Mor?" she asked.

I flinched. "Soon enough. Why don't you come to the bridge, see the sights of this lovely system?" I suggested.

"Why? It's just a bunch of stars and darkness. It's not the vacation that I was told I'd have," she lamented.

I fumed silently. Supernova Escapes may have failed me. They reassured me the Terran came with a perfect match to my genetic profile. I lifted from the seat and stepped toward the controls. No, I would not have this. My members throbbed excessively whenever I drew near to her.

"One moment," I said as I left her room.

"Out," I commanded the grunt sitting at the radio navigation console.

"But, Orxlon, we are approaching outer Mor," Tauxish stammered.

"Leave, I'll take care," I boomed.

The little Baedelion scurried off, griping under his breath. I'd deal with his insolence later. At the radio, the super transmitter lit up as the ship slowed. With the ship at cruising speed, I'd be able to contact Earth easily. Soon a voice came through; the voice crackling as it sounded out, but the reception was good enough.

"Perhaps you made a mistake with this one," I spoke deliberately under my breath.

"Orxlon, good to hear from you. How's it going?" Alex Tedleese asked. Alex played his Terran role very well, being a changeling from the Maklii System. He read a scant DNA profile from a Terran upon landing on Earth fifteen years ago and made himself into a full human, enough to fool the Terrans. Supernova Escapes hired him without question, and he served as my agent when I paid the hefty price for a Terran bride.

"She's unresponsive, belligerent even. I did not pay such a fee for a frosty reception from my future mate. Explain," I barked.

"Now, Orxlon, we gave you a pamphlet on Terran females. They aren't receptive and willing without a little coaxing. Try winning her with niceties, and she'll warm up to you soon," Alex replied.

"I don't know how to do that. Her pheromones are defective," I complained.

"No, she's perfect for you. Give it time. Remember, Terrans like it nice and sometimes slow," he said.

"I can't go slow. I'm not built to go slow. I want to claim her now, but she'd not be an agreeable partner." My jaw flexed as my teeth ground together. Just the thought of being next to her made my body ache with an unfettered desire.

"Trust me. Terrans have a sixth sense for their fated mates. Her desires for you will awaken. You need patience when dealing with her. Try being nice, I know it's not in your nature, but she will be more receptive to your savage side once she realizes you're meant for her." Alex promised.

"Very well. If she doesn't, I'm bringing her back to you and will expect a full refund and another Terran who will be more willing," I told him. I ended the communication before he could react and thrust the ship back into full flight, heading toward the dust rock, spinning with a furious dust typhoon on its surface.

I summoned Raven back to the bridge as we approached Mor. My arms tucked over my chest as I took deep breaths.

"Yes," she said.

"There it is." I nodded at the screen as we approached Mor.

She leaned in, peering at it. "What is that?" she asked.

"That is a dust typhoon," I replied. Lightning flashed from within it, twinkling. "And I will not land the *Remis* in that. If you are so bent on going back, I'll send you in a pod, and if you survive the landing, you can wait the weeks out until it lets up enough to radio out for a transport ship."

Her enormous eyes turned to me. "Weeks? You won't land there?"

"Certainly not, it would tear the ship apart," Bruns said as he stepped onto the bridge. My second in command stood nearly as tall as me, but was much older, his once black hair tinging blue-white.

"You don't... I'm not going there alone. What's the alternative?" she asked, her eyes set on Bruns this time.

"Not one. We can't stay here until that storm passes, we'll run out of fuel while powering life support on the ship and then possibly crash to the surface. We can fuel at Astavail. You were going there anyway," Bruns said. His bushy brow lifted.

"Okay," Raven replied.

She stuck around the bridge while we set coordinates to the Ovrabau System. After the conversation I had with Alex, I kept myself as pleasant as possible around Raven. She perched on the seat to my left, staring out the window.

"What made you go with the Supernova Escapes for your vacation?" I asked.

Tears filled her pretty eyes. "My parents loved traveling in space. They were on tour and their space transport crashed on Neptune's moon. I guess maybe I have a death wish, I don't know. Being on Earth is a constant reminder of what I've lost. I thought maybe it would refresh my spirit to travel outside the Terran System and see what's out here," she said.

I softened as I turned to her. "I understand losing one's family. I grew up amongst the debreu. My mother perished not long after I grew into a young boy. I barely remember her. A pandemic hit Salzoni and most of the females fell to it. My father took off leading a pack of angry Sleroirs to take back their homeland. I never saw him again." I shrugged.

"That's terrible. What are *debreus?*" It was the first time she ever spoke anything of tenderness toward me.

"It is like your foster child system. I grew up in a home of orphans. No matter. Most of the savages there got what they deserved. He abandoned me. He can rot," I said as I white knuckled the thruster controls. I hadn't thought about my father or my mother in a very long time. Now Raven had to cause my old memories to rise to the surface, and the anger I felt came crashing back. I shook it off. No time to dwell on the past. My future sat beside me, peering at me with sympathetic eyes. I had to take advantage. The urge to take her into my arms and carry her to my quarters grew stronger. I stood and advanced toward her.

Large brown eyes stared at me, her body relaxing, giving me the go ahead. I stooped, drawing closer to her as my hands moved to her arms. She didn't flinch. Instead, I felt a slight sigh. I couldn't take it as I leaned in, my lips meeting with hers. Shockingly, she didn't pull back. Instead, she moaned softly, her seam parting, pliable and wonderful. My tongue sought for her flavor, wanting to experience her. Three hearts pounded within my chest as I groaned and pulled her against me. The kiss taking on a fervor, driving me to the point of no return. Yet Alex's words floated in my head. *Take it slow. Have patience. She'll realize she's meant for you.* But has Raven realized it already? Her slight arms came to my broad shoulders, our lips moving together. My body was rocking to the edge of explosion. I groped her, feeling her pulse quicken against my body. Soft curves moved, pressed in, leaning more. Her lips opened, her tongue delighting with mine. Florin berries and Terran coffee hit my taste buds. I may try this drink. It will remind me of Raven. My body quivered with desire. I will make her mine, I will claim my mate. I paid for her, dearly. She's mine. I lifted her from her seat, her short stature taller when she stood than sitting, enabling me to stand more erect. She stood on her toes, reaching for me. Her body was warming under my touch. Yes! I will take her. I will claim her. She's my mate. We'll land on Astavail as mates. No denying it any longer. Terrans didn't need as much patience as Alex claimed. Raven's scent filled with pheromones that made my body yearn for her. I had to have her. I had to claim her before I exploded inside my pants.

I lifted my head for a moment and peered into her eyes. Strong desire flooded between us, her mammaries erecting the tiny nubs at their peaks, titillating me, teasing me. I wanted to taste each one. She smiled, her hands coming up to my jaw, pulling me to her again, her lips parting.

Chapter 3

RAVEN

What came over me I didn't quite understand. While part of me wanted to slap Orxlon, another part awoke and wanted to test what I felt. The desire within me flooded so quickly that I thought I'd lose myself. Yet, my hand quivered to deliver a slap right across that chiseled jaw. How dare he assume that I wanted a kiss? Though my body abandoned me, I pulled what little sense I had left and eased from his powerful embrace. His arms about me felt fabulous, those muscles tensing and moving against me. Images of his naked body coursed through my mind, almost too much. I wanted to see him naked. The giant bulge at his middle enticed me. Still, I didn't sign up for a vacation on another planet to have a fling with an *alien*. My parents taught me better than that. My parents. They were no longer alive. The ache in my heart pounded. Damn Orxlon for sparking desire in my body. Too long had I dreamt of finding *Mr. Right*. After my parents' sudden death just after I turned twenty-one, I froze. Earth held nothing but heartache for me. The men there only wanted a quick lay and pursuit of their careers, which held no place for me. Nope. I'm not on this vacation to find love, just peace of mind. This savage is trying to take advantage of me. I wouldn't let him, but he had me in his grasp. I struggled and yanked my arm free, my hand coming out and landing squarely across his jaw. He suddenly stepped back from me. A stark, angry expression exploded across his face, causing me to cower from his wrath.

"What was that for?" he asked. His hand came up to his jaw and rubbed it. I hit him hard, but not so hard as to do damage to his tough alien hide.

"The kiss. You had no right," I complained. Tears tried to fill my eyes, but I blinked them back as I tried to maintain my composure.

Orxlon stepped toward me again, his face etched in angst as he grabbed my arm. This time was not to pull me to him, but to pull me along behind him. I stumbled in his wake while he yanked. "Walk," he barked. The tender moment before was just a farce, probably so that he could score with a *Terran*. Asshole.

"What are you doing?" I demanded as he shoved me into the room.

"You act like a savage, so we'll treat you like one," he replied.

"Savage?" I laughed. "Seems that you're the savage taking advantage of me."

"You're a tease. I won't have insubordination on my ship. Those who threaten me and fight against me receive just punishment. Until we land on Astavail, this is your place," he told me.

"Wait!" I yelled as he stepped to the door. I ran to him. He didn't flinch back, but no wonder, he's like a full foot taller than me, and his muscle mass overshadows me three times over.

"What?" His teeth ground.

"Why are you locking me in here? Just because I slapped you, because you kissed me?"

"Yes. You acted like you enjoyed it until that slap. I don't understand you. Locking you in here is as much for your safety as it is for your punishment. I can't control myself around you. If you don't want me grabbing you and kissing you again, then you're better off to stay locked inside this room," he replied as he strode out the door. It shut and locked.

I paced the floor after trying the door and found it securely locked. What did he mean by locking me in here for my safety? And would he kiss me again? My body tingled at the thought. I should slap my face for even entertaining the idea. The thought of Orxlon's pulsing muscles and iron grip intrigued me. That bulge. Oh my. I shook my head. I couldn't entertain such thoughts, could I? My fists ground the tears that formed as I stomped to the bunk and flung myself on top of the covers. The pillow provided a nice comfort as I hugged it tightly and faced the wall. Only, I couldn't lay there for long. I was angry and intrigued at the same time. Delighted, yet scared. What the hell was wrong with me? So many conflicting thoughts rushed through my head, faster than I could keep up. My emotions flowed like the turns and hills of a rollercoaster ride. I kept the pillow in my embrace. Pulling my legs up, I relaxed in a fetal position. I rocked and stared out into nothing as I tried to make sense of my racing mind. I rolled until I eventually sat up on top of the bed.

The walls closed in on me as I rocked on my bottom. It was too small a space for a long period of time. I don't like traveling on small ships, where there is no room to really stretch out and breathe. Swallowing hard, I counted. My eyes closed, I took deep breaths which helped for a moment, but as soon as I opened my eyes, my body shook. I gulped air; the breaths coming in fast and short, until I was gasping.

"Please, help me," I cried. "Oh, please, I can't do this." Tears streamed down my face as I struggled with my breathing. The room spun as lightheadedness caused my vision to blur. My cries resounded loudly inside my ears, but the hissing was louder. Gasping and crying, I couldn't control it.

Suddenly, the door opened and Orxlon rushed in toward me. He perched on the bed and his enormous arms wrapped around me.

"Raven, are you okay? What's wrong?"

I answered with sobs and gasps. He kept stroking my long hair, soothing me. "It's okay, shhh, I'm here." Ironically, my body reacted to his kindness. The gasps settled, my breathing steadied. I took slow deep breaths, my racing heart finally slowed to normal. For a long moment, I rested against him, feeling his powerful heartbeat. It soothed me and relaxed my nerves. My eyes closed as the heaviness of fatigue grasped me. For a split second, I fell asleep! I grew so comfortable that I lost consciousness. Not as in passing out, but as in feeling content, relaxed. I hadn't felt that way since I left Earth. His hand stroked my hair and massaged my shoulders. He didn't make a move on me other than to let me rest. To my surprise, I enjoyed feeling his heart beating. I enjoyed his muscular arms wrapped around me. Orxlon gave me a comfort beyond my understanding, which confused me. Finally, I lifted from him and offered a slight smile.

"Are you okay?" His genuine concern touched me.

I nodded. "I'm sorry. I had a panic attack. I'm in unfamiliar territory and I can't handle being locked up. As a small child, I had panic attacks when confined on a train sleeper compartment. My parents tried to keep me from being in small enclosures after that."

"Little Terran, you gave me a scare. Grufss heard you crying and fetched me. I rushed in here. But I felt your vitals calm as I held you, so I just kept holding you. Do you realize I've been in here like this for more than an hour?" He peered into my eyes, his golden orbs filled with sincerity.

"You have? I know that I shut my eyes, but I didn't think I had slept that long," I replied.

"Yes, and I didn't want to interrupt you. I'm sorry this has been such a difficult journey for you so far. I'm trying to behave with you. You must understand, Salzonians differ from Terrans in the way we approach some things," he told me.

Orxlon's words confused me. Why did he care to tell me this? My heart stirred in his presence and it shook me in a strange way. My hand moved up along his muscular bicep, which flexed beneath my touch. "You're a mass of muscles," I told him. My cheeks grew hot at how I expressed this out loud. What was wrong with me? The emotions churned within me; something had sparked to life and yet I couldn't quite grasp what it was. Was I attracted to the brute? I had sworn that I'd never fall for an alien like I'd seen some women on Earth do. Some movie stars had giant brutes on their arms at the red carpet ceremonies. I always laughed about it, but after getting so close to Orxlon, I came to understand the appeal.

"I can't stay locked away in this room. I still don't completely understand why you locked me away like this, but please understand when these panic attacks hit, I lose control of myself," I advised.

He smiled and nodded. "I fear losing control of myself being around you. In case you haven't noticed, I have a fierce attraction to you."

"I guess that makes a little sense. I mean, on Earth the males don't come at us like this most of the time," I replied.

"I'm not a Terran. Salzonians react differently to the opposite sex when they meet one they... Well, when they meet one they are attracted to."

I smiled at him. "So, you find me attractive. That's odd that you're reacting like this, like I'm your long lost soulmate or something."

Orxlon flinched and looked away quickly. "Perhaps. When a Salzonian meets one he believes to be his mate, certain biological things occur. You've awoken the beast inside me, I'm afraid," he said as he grinned. His large blocky teeth beamed at me, sparkling white. I would have liked to have known what kind of toothpaste he used.

My body trembled at his words. "*Beast?* Like you're a

savage and will harm me in the name of mating?"

He chuckled, a low, deep reverberation emitting that soothed me. "Possibly. I can't help it. Strong urges have formed inside me and I have a powerful desire for you. Do you feel it too?"

His words shook me. Did I? Maybe, though it went against everything I believed or thought possible. "Um, I don't know. I'm confused. I'm a little afraid of you. I'm not sure that I want you to claim me like that. I don't know," I told him honestly.

"Sir, we're at the realm of Astavail," Grufss suddenly said at the doorway to the room. "You're needed on the bridge."

"Please, don't lock me in here again," I begged as he stood to his feet.

Chapter 4

ORXLON

"The surface appears clear," Bruns said as the ship orbited around Astavail.

I peered out the window at the lush green and indigo blue planet. I had to make good on the ruse and bring Raven to the paradise spot. If she suspected Supernova Escapes was really an alien bridal agency, she'd never trust me. At least we could land here so that she'd spend a few days bathing in the orange glow star light and then she'd realize her genuine feelings for me. I could very well claim my mate on the surface, on a bed of *stagarsh moss* at the surf's edge.

"Pull up heat signatures, let's go around once more, and carefully scan the surface. We know the Dausers have come here before. We can't risk running into them," I told my crew.

"On screen," Bruns replied.

Before us, the surface of Astavail formed in three dimensions, the lush jungles providing a cooling cover to anything beneath the canopy. "Could be something under there," I told him.

"Astavail is teeming with life, sir. It's hard to tell..."

"No, we'd see definite formations of intelligent beings. No beings of higher intelligence are on Astavail, which is why the Agency offered it as a paradise get-away for the Terran. She chose it because of the open spaces." I realized that she had chosen it because of her claustrophobic tendency. I couldn't blame her, knowing how she had reacted to being locked inside her room.

Grufss approached the bridge. "No answer to the hails, sir," he told me.

"What is Raven doing?" I had given Grufss the job of keeping tabs on my Terran mate.

"She's wandering the halls, sir. She keeps eyeing this direction, but hesitates to step this way."

"Hmm." My hand landed on my chest, my three hearts beating in rhythm. It was an unfamiliar sensation, as I've lived my entire life with the three of them out of sync until meeting Raven. Yes, I'll claim her as my mate. Only a true mate could do that to a Salzonians' hearts. I smiled at evolution for allowing us a chance at procreation while having a mate by my side. Deep inside, my libido throbbed for attention, for release. I had to quell it for now and give more time to bring Raven into my trust. She wanted me, of that much I was certain.

"Strap in for landing," I belted into the comm. The ship's landing alarm sounded, and every live body scampered for a seat. I hoped Grufss took care of Raven and had her sit in her chair as well.

"Hold off for a moment," I said as I strode off the bridge in search of Raven. She was sitting tentatively in her room, her mouth turned down as her hopeless eyes took me in when I stepped inside her room.

"Come with me," I said to her.

"Why? Where?"

"I am the captain of this ship. My passengers and crew do as I command. Come with me," I barked.

She flinched, but stood anyway. I motioned for her to follow and offered a smile. She rose from her chair and followed me, looking scared as we stepped toward the bridge.

"Sit," I said as I motioned at the seat next to mine. "We're about to land on Astavail, and I want you to experience it from the bridge."

"Oh, nice," Raven said as her countenance became more friendly while she adjusted the straps over her petite body.

Astavail appeared quiet and restful until we entered the atmosphere. Turbulence from the ever changing magnetic poles caused the *Remis* to shudder upon impact, the ground speeding at us far too quickly.

"Brace for impact," I shouted.

Raven gasped. Bruns grunted as he clamored for the manual controls, and I squeezed on the landing gear to allow for a slide instead of a nice setdown. The gear ground into the atmosphere as the great ship shuddered. Flames flashed from around the hull and the reactor suddenly malfunctioned, causing us to burn through the atmosphere without the ship's shields on full power.

"Hold on!" I gripped the throttle and pulled back hard as the ship hit the ground, trees and great stones slowing our speed, but not enough to stop us from flipping straight into a large sand embankment. The nose of the

craft dug deep into Astavail, while the ship groaned and halted. We clung to our seats at the steep angle.

"Raven, stay put!" I cut myself loose and fell into the bridge console, my full weight keeping me upright. Bruns did the same.

"Report!" I shouted into the comm.

Small grunts and affirmations came from the rest of the ship. "Report, *Remis*," I shouted to the scrolling lights above the window.

"Ship sustained damage. The hull is intact, but structurally fatigued. The reactor is at 45%, with several mainline breakers tripped." The ship's AI spoke in a calm voice while reading off the report from its scan.

"Is it repairable?"

"With proper retooling, a new hull covering, and reactor repair, yes."

Raven whimpered as she stared at me. "Anyone hurt?" I asked on the comm.

A few reports filtered in of bumps and bruises. The ship's doctor, Evers'blx, would be busy helping the crew. I needed to get Raven off the ship before she went into a panic attack again.

"Hold on to me," I said as I cut her free from the straps. She fell immediately into my arms and clung to my neck. A soft, warm flutter rushed through my chest, a surge of energy struck me to save the frail human. My instincts were correct to have her with me during the landing, her room bent at a sharp angle and the chair loosened from the floor. She wouldn't have survived the impact.

"That was nuts," Raven said as she stumbled away

from the ship.

"Magnetic turbulence in the atmosphere caused it." I shook my head. The ship's nose stuck deep into Astavail as the large vessel spat out her occupants. At least everyone survived, though a few had bumps and bruises.

"Okay, crew, can we fix this?"

"I've radioed to Vestra for help. They will be here in a few days," Bruns responded.

"A few days." I nodded and looked over at my soon-to-be mate. Her enormous eyes scanned the landscape fearfully. I sensed her small heart beating hard inside her chest.

"It's going to be alright," I said as I stepped toward her.

"Sir, we aren't alone," Bruns said as he handed me the scanner.

"Put the ship into stealth and stay onboard and out of range as best you can until help arrives," I said before I turned to Raven.

"What?"

"It's the Dausers. We aren't alone. We need to get away from the wreckage and find a place to hide until they repair the ship," I said as I grabbed her hand and tugged her in the opposite direction of the camp we had spotted on our scanners.

"Wait, I'm here to vacation," Raven said as she pulled away from me.

"Shhhh, if they hear you they will grab you. The Dausers are a rival to Salizonis. They'd just as soon kill us as to share a planet with us," I informed the Terran woman.

"*My* vacation. I came here to relax and enjoy myself. I don't care what happens with the *Remis*. Help will arrive in several days. You can stick with your ship," she said as she traipsed away from me.

"You can't! Where will you go?" I asked as I quickly went after her. The urge to grab her and run struck strong, but I didn't want to make her weary of me again.

"I... don't know. I thought this place would have a resort. I mean, Supernova Escapes promised a wonderful vacation."

"Did you pay for this, or did you win it?" I asked in order to remind her.

"Well, I won it. I submitted for a drawing and they said I won a seat on the Starlight Express to Astavail. But the Starlight Express dropped me on Mor. Then, you showed up." Her words slowed as she gazed at me. "Wait a minute. I didn't win a vacation, did I?" Her head shook.

"You did, but not as you had expected. I'll explain it later, but first we need to hide. If they find the ship, they'll commandeer it. I don't want you anywhere near it until it's ready to fly out," I told her.

"I have no choice, do I?"

"No, you will need to come with me. I won't hurt you, I promise," I said as I took her hand and led her deep into the jungle. Raven didn't say a word as we ran, dodging the giant vines and plet trees. Little critters scurried along in front of us.

When we slowed, I let go of her, giving her the chance to stick with me without having to hold her hand.

"Please explain why I'm here if I didn't really win an exotic vacation," she said.

"What you need to understand is that Supernova Escapes operates as a space age travel agency. They do offer vacations, from what I understand. The vacation you signed up to win isn't really a vacation like you probably expected," I answered.

"I gathered that a few minutes ago." She frowned as we walked.

"Your blood gave the agency your genetic map, and they put it in a database of those who are looking for mates. We use Supernova Escapes as a mate location agency."

"*Seriously?*" Raven stopped, her hand on her hip as she glared at me. "I did not sign up for a matchmaking service. They said the blood was to make sure that I could travel to other systems in the galaxy, not to match my DNA with aliens! So what does this mean? Did you sign up looking for a bride?"

My eyes closed as I bowed my head. "Yes. But you need to understand, it's not what you expect, at least not with me."

"Not what I expect? Exactly what does that mean?"

"Some who seek a Terran bride claim them without their consent."

Raven backed away from me until she hit a tree. Her hand came out as her eyes widened. "Is that your intent? To *claim* me?"

Calm. My body shuddered inwardly as I focused on speaking the right words. "I signed up for a genetic match, yes, I want a mate. My genetic profile perfectly matched yours. I won't claim you without your consent though," I promised, though I wasn't sure I'd be able to keep that promise. It took all the restraint I had to keep from grabbing her and throwing her on the ground to claim her right there.

"I'm not, no. That won't happen. Don't even think that it will. I didn't agree to any of this. I just want to go back to Earth," Raven told me as she shook her head.

A noise in the distance caused me to hold up my hand for her to be quiet. Something lurked in the shadows. We had to move quickly.

"Silence. We need to keep going until we find a safe hiding place," I quietly said. I took her hand. The conversation was over for now.

Chapter 5

The beast ran with me through the dense jungle. My head and heart reeled from his confession. I hadn't won a vacation; I had won an alien groom. While I feared him, I found the information intriguing. It put a whole new spin to my naughty thoughts about him, knowing that we were perfectly matched. But to have him claim me, as if I were his property, as if it were his *right?* I don't think so. As beefy and sexy as he was, being claimed wasn't my style.

Sharp hills and craggy valleys made for rough travel on foot. I wore a pair of space chugs, which were not really meant for hiking through rough terrain. I thought I'd be relaxing on the beach, with a tall spindly alien serving me exotic fruit drinks while I enjoyed the indigo surf and the beautiful emerald green dusk. Orxlon kept looking behind us whenever we paused and he'd listen. I heard nothing, but his ears twitched. I didn't question it. Alien bodies differed from human ones.

My white shoes were stained with dark green from the thick grass growing in patches, where the green-yellow light hit through the thick canopy of leaves from above. Why did I choose white? Why didn't I purchase the standard space boots, the ones with traction soles that would help on planets where the gravity was lacking? White matched everything that I planned to wear on this exotic Astavail vacation. Unfortunately, there was no vacation and my heart fluttered at the implications of that.

I stopped as I bent over, catching my breath. "We need to go back. My bags are still on the *Remis*," I said. I needed a change of clothes, and I'd like to change shoes.

"What? Um, *no!* Your bags are fine on the ship. Don't you understand what we're doing here? The Dausers are savage beasts," he argued.

"And you aren't?" Maybe I'd like to try my chances with them over him. Orxlon ordered me around as a mail order bride and I stepped into it willingly, though unknowingly.

"Not like they are. You haven't even laid eyes on their kind. They will view you as a prize worthy of Trijun's Auctions. Now, if you want to be a sex slave, let them have you," he growled.

"You want that from me," I spat as I glared at him.

"I don't want to enslave you," he countered. He didn't deny the sex part and my eyes slid to his well-packed mid-section. Why did I have the urge to check him out like he was a beach boy from back home? He chuckled as I floundered. He caught me staring!

I jerked my eyes away, averting them to the jungle floor. "You paid for me. It's just the same, isn't it?"

"No, I didn't pay for a sex slave. I paid for a Terran bride, for a mate. Now come on, we'll deal with the details of that later. We need to find a hidden shelter before nightfall," Orxlon pleaded.

My feet carried me over the rough terrain as his hand held tightly to mine to force me to keep up with him. Why didn't he just throw me over his shoulder and run? It wouldn't be much for him to lift me, like he did on the crashed ship earlier. My fingers tingled as the desire to touch his muscled arms rushed through me.

Stop it, Raven! I had to get hold of myself. Thinking along these lines would do neither of us any good. Besides, I didn't want him to claim me. *Did I?*

"Here, ahead," he suddenly said as he pulled at me.

I looked forward and saw nothing but the dense green leaves before us. Though the sun was quickly sinking over the horizon, the odd green dusk made it damn impossible to see anything through the trees and shrubs. Yet we rushed ahead anyway with purpose. His eyes focused on something and when we emerged from the woods we found a great creek that ran below. The sound of it was muffled somewhat from the walls of the small canyon. Before us, a waterfall sprayed, and we dove into it, the water rushing over us, soaking us from head to toe.

"Stop it!" I shouted as he continued to pull me along, but Orxlon didn't listen. We emerged inside a cave hidden behind the waterfall. The entrance was small when compared to the room on the ship itself, about as large as the bedroom I had in my apartment on Earth; the apartment I had left behind and probably would never see again.

The waterfall drowned my racing thoughts as I wandered around the length of the cave, looking for a corridor or an entrance into a larger area, but there was none. Dark and dank, the cave walls seemed to close in on me. Try as I might, I couldn't keep my breath from growing ragged. My eyes swung toward the water rushing over the entrance. What if these barbarian aliens came through? We'd have no escape. I had always looked for exits in any room that I entered. I chose the apartment back home because it had a nice back door. With two ways of leaving the place, I didn't feel as closed in as I would in other places. But in this cave, the walls came together.

"It's okay, hey, you're not locked in here," Orxlon said as his gigantic hand rubbed down my back.

My mouth dried and saliva wouldn't form. I gasped for air as the confines closed in on me. Orxlon pulled me to him, his arms encircling me. It didn't make me feel more claustrophobic, but soothed me. He perched on a large rock in the middle, and drew me onto his lap, his hand rubbing down my back. Strangely, my nerves calmed with his touch. I didn't shrink back, even while knowing that this savage alien wanted to claim me. Instead, I leaned into him, resting my head on his very powerful shoulders.

As my breathing softened, I reared my head back and peered into the glowing orbs of his eyes. The odd two moons rose in the sky, casting a faint emerald glow over the area. The water danced at the door, sending shards of green light, giving us a show.

"I'm sorry. I don't know why I can't control this," I said. I stayed on his lap, because somehow it made me feel safe and whole.

"It's okay. I could sense that you were beginning to panic. We have a way out of here, so please don't fret," he told me calmly.

I glanced at the glowing entrance. "We don't if those Dausers come through the waterfall."

"Chances are they don't know about this cave. We're safe inside here and well-hidden. We'll wait here until morning and then find a better hiding place, as far away from their camp as possible until the crew repairs the *Remis*."

"I'm fine now," I said as I crawled from his lap. The big brute wasn't so bad, but I didn't want to be so close to him.

"Look, I'll protect you. You need to understand something about me. I realize how well the agency matched us," Orxlon told me.

I shook my head and walked to the opposite side of the cave. "No, I don't want to hear about it. I'm not your mate. I'm not something you can just claim and then be yours forever," I said.

His face fell, the corners of his mouth turned down as he nodded slightly, and turned from me. His keen eyes peered at the rushing water as if looking through it.

"I need to check the surrounding area. Stay here," he commanded as he pushed through the water.

The rock in the center of the cave held little comfort. I missed being on the *Remis* locked inside the tiny room. Anything was better than this dank, dark cave. Still, Orxlon had a way of calming me that even I didn't understand. I shivered. Cold dampness filtered in and surrounded me. My arms did little to ease the shivers, so I stood and walked. To leave the place, I would have had to step through the water, which I didn't want to do. My clothing dried quickly, thanks to the new materials created specifically for space travel. Lightweight and fast dry. I wish I had my bags, though. Why didn't I insist on bringing them off the ship?

Twenty-two steps. My feet paced back and forth as I counted, cursing the fact that I wore white shoes. Twenty-one steps from the waterfall to the back of the cave. Twenty-four steps if I walked diagonally taking long strides.

"Orxlon?" I called from the entrance. I strained to hear whether he responded. No answer came back from him as deafening water rushing over the small falls. He'd gone a while ago, too long for my comfort. What if something had happened to him? I mean, he was a big, beefy being, but even he could fall and hurt himself. Unless he had some sort of healing magic, that is. I believed in the possibilities of magic. Orxlon had some sort of means to calm me, even when his touch should have made me feel much worse. Yet, I sat on his large lap for a while, the feeling of sleepiness washing over me. Where was he?

The moons moved beyond the cave entrance, leaving me in pitch blackness. Suddenly, something came through the water. I cowered back against the cave wall, fearful of it being a Dauser.

"Raven? Are you alright?" Orxlon's voice approached. Great. He could see in the dark too as water droplets landed on me.

"I'm fine," I said, probably too curtly.

"We can rest for the night. There are shorter days and nights here than on Earth. That can be both good and bad. It means less sleep for a Terran who needs eight hours, yet good because at first light we can leave to find better shelter. Or, at the very least, we can make this place more comfortable for you," he told me.

"I'm not sure this place can be made comfortable, but I'm fine. We should take turns sleeping, and keep watch, in case something creeps in this way," I said as I yawned. Dammit, I wanted the first watch so that I could find a way to escape.

"I'll take first watch," he said to me as he positioned himself at the entrance of the cave.

I nodded. Fatigue won out as I sat against the rock, and though my body screamed from lack of cushion, my heavy eyes closed and I welcomed sleep.

Deep in my mind, fitful dreams formed against my better judgement. So much had happened after leaving Earth that I couldn't easily process it. I missed my life on Earth despite the heartache of losing my parents. I had a safe apartment, the basic comforts of home and all the clothing and shoes I wanted. Something deep within my being urged me to try for the Supernova Escapes vacation. I should have known better. It had been too good to be true, which was what some of my friends back home told me when I entered the contest. How lucky was I that I had won? Here I was, in a cold, damp cave with an alien who wanted to claim me as his mate.

Chapter 6

ORXLON

Raven hesitated to trust me fully. Her posture stiffened when I came around aside from when I helped her through the panic attacks. A complicated creature. She had stolen my hearts. My hand rested on my chest, the solid *thump, thump, thump* within assuring me Supernova Escapes hit it right by sending her to me. The need to take her to a safe place to live and thrive became my top priority. Damn ruse of winning a paradise vacation. Landing on Astavail only kept her from finding out the truth until the right moment.

Raven's countenance softened as she relaxed and sleep took her. There was no way that I would wake her to take watch. For one, her eyes and ears held nothing to the fine-tuned capabilities of mine. Something stirred outside on the left. I tensed, ready to strike. *No!* I wouldn't allow anything to happen to my mate. Without another thought, I bound through the falls, ready to draw the enemy away.

Dausers, like me, could see well in the dark. My advantage of surprise held over them as I made my way above the falls. They came near, their bumbling legs carrying them with a herald of noise. The opened river above the cave shimmered in the moons' light, possibly revealing my presence. Walking upstream, I'd make my way around to the other side and draw them away somehow. My precious Terran slept well, her brain in deep sleep, my senses keeping check on her. Raven didn't realize that my hearts had tuned into her on the ethereal level. I felt what she felt, whether scared or startled or peacefully sleeping. The river slowed, the massive stones allowing me to step across unnoticed.

I came back around as fast as I could while remaining in the background, hiding among the shadows. One heart lurched out of sync with the others. The Dausers surrounded the falls, removing their coverings. Fat rolls of flesh glistened as the water cooled them. It was too hot in the humid atmosphere of Astavail, so they sought opportunities to cool their bodies. I watched from the shadows. They didn't know about Raven, or they would have already crashed through the falls after her. The water, thankfully, covered her scent, masking it fully. Astavail held many creatures that emitted pungent odors, probably foreign to their olfactory nerves.

My hearts beat out of rhythm. I no longer felt Raven's heart or her emotions. Had she awoken? Would she be able to see or hear the enemy so close? I held my breath when one of them made his way to the falls and dipped his head into the water. He needed only to push through to see the cave. Surely, they would want to explore it and would discover the hidden Terran within, her small body asleep inside.

The Dauser backed away, barking an order at a grunt on the bank. My teeth clenched as I listened.

"Bring our supplies, we'll camp here. Plenty of water

and it's cooler down here," he said.

Concerned by their presence, I paced my breath as my body prepared to jump forward to fight for my mate. They outnumbered me and if they saw a Salzonian in their midst they wouldn't think twice about slitting my throat. No, I couldn't do that. I could go back to the *Remis* and risk losing Raven. We ran quickly through the jungle the previous day, covering a long distance, but I could find my way back easily. However, what if they discovered her before I returned? She'd not understand their distinctive dialect and language. Her implant was calibrated to my language by design.

Another dove into the pool and swam toward the falls. Why did they do things at night? I was thankful that Raven was probably still sleeping through this. I had to come up with a diversion to draw them away, though. Looking around, I found saplings growing in a small grove behind me. They were perfect for starting fires. The small trees yanked from the dirt easily as I gathered as many as I could carry. The larger sap grove grew tall, the goo dripping down each tree. Small creatures scurried around me.

"Sorry, leave or you'll die," I said to the little ones all around my feet as I made a trail of saplings from behind the grove leading to one tree in the middle. It would ignite easily, causing a blaze that would draw their attention away from the cave.

I ran forward, checking what the enemy was doing at that point. One appeared from the falls. He had stepped through.

"It's a cave. Perhaps we should use it," he said to the

others.

"No time. There are caves all over the place. We camp and we leave at first light," the leader replied.

But he didn't stop moving toward the falls. He rushed ahead, diving through the raging water. I jumped back and struck a flint stone against another rock, and it sparked. The trail of sap and saplings lit immediately. I jumped out of the way as the flames leapt through the jungle floor and toward the sap grove.

"*Fire!* Quick, it could be one of our engines," the leader said.

I smiled. Perfect. Let them think their craft had caused it. They scrambled away, coming fast from the falls. Once they had left the pool and rushed toward the blaze, I flung myself quickly toward Raven. I reached the falls in moments and rushed through the water. Raven flung herself into my arms, her breathing labored. My three hearts calmed and beat in unison once again.

"Where did you go?" she cried.

"I heard them approaching. I went out to create a diversion to draw them away. It worked!" I held her tightly in my arms.

"I woke up and couldn't see, but I heard them. I worried that they had caught you. I didn't know what to do. This cave has no place to hide," she stammered.

"Two came in. Did they see you?" I held my breath.

"No. I laid behind the rock and flattened myself against the floor. They didn't come in all the way," she answered.

"You did the right thing," I replied as I stroked her

hair. That seemed to calm her more than anything else could.

"What if they had captured me? What then?" Raven asked as she looked up at me. Her eyes were wide and searching. The sun began to rise, casting a bright yellow-green light through the waterfall.

"They didn't. We don't need to think about the *what ifs*. But come on, we need to find another place to hide. They didn't discover you or me and hopefully they have not seen the *Remis*." I stood and took hold of her frail hand which pulsed inside mine.

"Where are we going?"

"I saw another cave upriver. Their travel trajectory isn't in that direction. We'll be safer there," I told Raven, though not too convincingly.

"How do you know where they're going?"

"I don't, exactly. But they know about this place. I'm not certain where they are trying to go, but I heard them talk about traveling through."

"You understood them?"

"Unfortunately."

"No, *fortunately*. I can understand you, but I can't even understand the others on your ship," she worried.

"I know. Your implant is for my language only," I admitted.

"Of course." Raven's lips formed a tight, straight line.

"Let's go before they head back," I said.

We hopped from the cave entrance through the falls. The fire burned in the distance and I hoped that it wouldn't ignite the surrounding jungle. Being that it was damp, I hoped it would just burn out. The Dausers had disappeared beyond the fire already. I grabbed Raven's hand, and we clamored up the embankment to the top of the falls on the other side and made our way upstream.

"Wait, perhaps they won't come back," I thought out loud.

"Look," Raven said as she pointed. Sure enough, the Dausers were coming back and carrying large crates on napalops. The large animals ambled along slowly.

"What is that?"

"It's a napalop. They are native to Astavail. They do the same things as horses on Earth. Quick, we need to hide. There is no way the napalop will fit into the cave entrance." I took her hand again as we slid back down the embankment and rushed through the falls and into the cave.

"We'll stop here and let them rest," the leader said just outside the cave.

"What are they..."

"*Shhhh,*" I said to Raven, so that I could hear them.

"The water's cool here, unlike on top," the Dauser told his comrades.

A low growl came from me as I shook my head.

"What?" Raven whispered as her small hand clutched my arm. I forget that she couldn't see or hear the others as I could.

"They are staying here for a time," I told her. My jaw flexed as I ground my teeth together. We needed food and better comfort, especially for the Terran.

"What will we do?" Raven's voice verged on panic.

I turned to face her. I couldn't allow her to fill with

panic again. Her gasping and cries were not quiet. I pulled her into my arms and embraced her tightly. Her body began to relax.

"We'll think of something," I promised quietly.

I held Raven until her pulse lowered once again. Her body relaxed as she nodded, her arms dropping from me.

"I'm scared, Orxlon. Please don't leave me again."

My hearts soared. Raven wanted me to stay with her, even if it meant keeping the company of a beast. "I don't plan to," I told her as I looked into her eyes. Her stomach growled.

"I guess I'm hungry," she told me.

"I'll sneak out and get some food for us," I replied.

"No! Don't leave me. If you leave, I'm leaving, even if it is for food. I can drink the water, and I already have."

"It's okay, the water is drinkable," I confirmed.

"Good. It hasn't made me sick yet, so I figured as much. But I want off this horrible planet as soon as possible," she said.

"I want to take you off here too."

Raven stared into my eyes, her sad face searching my soul. "If only you'd have been honest with me from the beginning," she told me.

"And what does that mean?"

"I mean, I thought I was going on a solo vacation. I don't know, maybe if you had been honest when I first boarded your ship we would be here. It's not a nice way to meet someone you want to date."

I winced. *Date?* "Blame it on Supernova Escapes. I've heard other Terrans who ended up being very satisfied with their vacations," I said as I grinned.

This time she winced. "It would be nice to have a choice. I don't feel as if I ever had a choice. It was a ruse. A lie," she complained.

"What if you discovered the truth sooner? Would you have run from me?" I held my breath, waiting for her answer.

She smiled sweetly. "Maybe not, but we'll never know, will we?" At least Raven was relaxed and admitted that she was not completely repulsed by me.

Chapter 7

RAVEN

The brute paced in front of the entrance, listening through the deafening water. I couldn't hear anything, but I could see the shadows of his sworn enemy just beyond. Oh, how I wished this had turned out differently. Some anger bubbled within me at the entire experience. I was tricked. The agency tricked me. Orxlon tricked me. Like I'm not able to decide about what I want. No one before had ever forced me to do something that I didn't want to do. And just to prove a point, if someone tried to do as much, I'd do the opposite of what they wanted. I didn't sign up for this. Maybe if we hadn't crashed onto the planet and I could have relaxed on a beach; maybe I'd have given Orxlon a second look. He made too many assumptions about me, and it pissed me off.

We settled behind the giant rock in the center of the cave. I let him place his arm around me and let him think that he protected me. I wondered about the Dausers. They hated Orxlon's people. Perhaps there was a good reason. Perhaps they knew his people did nefarious things like kidnapping and lying to a Terran to claim her. The more I thought about it, the more I wanted to run from him. Still, his presence somehow made me feel better. He could have left me here to die. He could have sent me careening back onto Mor in a pod left to perish in the dust typhoon. He didn't. Orxlon very much seemed to believe that I was his mate. My eyes strained to see his form resting beside me. His deep breathing showed that he dreamed as he slept and that he probably would not rouse easily. This wasn't surprising, considering he had had no sleep since being on the *Remis* before the crash. My heart stirred. Out of sorrow? Out of pity?

It grew quiet outside and Orxlon rolled away, a soft snore on his lips. I took the chance and stole toward the entrance. The moons lit the area, but there was only an eerie wail of whatever night birds flew in the area that reached my ears. I didn't think too long about my next move. I took a chance and leapt through the waters, emerging on the other side.

I paused, listening. Nothing stirred save for the wailers in the trees above. They paid me no mind as I gingerly stepped away from the cave. I just had to see for myself. For all I knew, the Dausers worked with Orxlon in making me think that we were in danger. No aliens appeared to be encamped near the falls, as Orxlon had claimed. Shivers rushed through my body. It was not a reaction from being cold, but from the anger inside me. I tiptoed away, knowing that he had ears that could probably hear for miles.

The trail leading up the embankment emerged next to the gentle river. The serene beauty pushed me onward as I followed the trail made by Astavail's game, if there were such animals around. I kept walking and walking and never saw another cave like Orxlon described. I bet he lied about that too. I wanted to go in the opposite direction of the Dausers and of the *Remis*. I decided to trust my instincts, which propelled me to cut off the path and head out of the thick jungle. There, the density of the trees would allay and make for easier walking. How dare an alien capture me and lie to me only to claim me when he felt the urge. My body tingled at the thought. Shaking my head, I kept walking. Just because the alien had muscles that wouldn't quit didn't mean I should go for him. That was too materialistic of a thought. What if claiming me put a mark on me I could never shake? He'd want me to bear his young. No, I wouldn't allow for it, even though the tingling inside me wouldn't stop. A part of me felt sorry for him, but the stronger part of me kept my feet going, away from the cave.

When did the thick trees return? The sun edged up; the place grew unfamiliar. Wide, gnarled trunks blocked my path as I forged ahead, hoping to find an opening. Pausing, I looked around. It looked the same in all directions. The wailers had stopped, probably hiding in their nests until nightfall. Creatures came alive, calling and slithering, and running, and moving unseen. No doubt they watched me as I scampered along, trying to figure out how to get out of the thick, wild jungle. I ducked behind such a tree when a gallop came very near. Something very large and on bumbling legs. When it receded, I found the footprints. It had huge hooves, big enough for both of my feet to fit inside and then some. A shiver raced down my spine. I'd rather be with Orxlon right now than lost here in the jungle. I'd walked for hours. The jungle looked the same in every direction that I turned. I should have paid attention when I read about Astavail and learned the direction of the sun. *Stupid girl.*

The sound of rustling caused me to pause for a moment. The familiar gargle of the Dausers reached my ears. An enormous tree offered a small dip beneath it, the roots growing upward, giving me a place to hide. Pungent soil surrounded me as I nestled under the large roots and prayed that the aliens wouldn't walk around the tree. To camouflage myself, I pulled the blackened dirt over my white shoes, cringing inside as I dirtied myself further. Overhead, the sky rumbled. It's a jungle, susceptible to daily storms. Fat drops of water pelted the ground sporadically until the deluge dropped. Mother nature on Astavail showed her cruelty until little streams of water flowed, filling the dip under the tree, the roots gulping in the hydration, while I only hoped that I wouldn't drown.

Dark clouds hid the sun, the area suddenly shrouded in deep shadows. Dausers pranced about as if this were their ideal environment. Maybe so. I caught a glimpse of them as they stepped closer to the tree in which I hid. Maybe the rain had hidden my scent. Maybe they didn't have a keen sense of smell at all. I could only hope. Their fat bellies jiggled under the tunics and the belts they wore which held weapons and daggers strapped to their torso. I knew that I couldn't step out as I hunkered inside the slimy mudhole. My clothes and shoes would never be the same. Why did I leave him? Orxlon wasn't so bad. He had a thing for me and claimed that our DNA matched. Maybe he was right. He had a strange way to calm me, which I missed. A shiver rushed through my body and puckered skin appeared on the palms of my hands. No, I couldn't lose it out here in the alien rain. Tears ran down my face.

When a fat, lumbering critter appeared that looked very much like a hog from Earth, a Dauser lurched forward quickly. His dagger flashed as it thrust into the creature, which shrieked. My hands covered my ears as I watched. Instead of killing the poor creature, they laughed as they let it go, and it, too weak to run, became their entertainment. A poker, which had been in the fire pit they lit, was poked at it. The shrieking came again, it's purple blue blood oozing from the dagger wound, and where the poker had landed, a large welt appeared. I felt sorry for the creature. I could understand the need for food, but to injure it and play with it was just cruel.

When they finally slit the creature's throat, the shrieking stopped. First, they drained the blood and shared it, drinking the thick liquid. It dripped from their fat chins as they tore into the hide, pulling it apart and tossing it into a pot on the fire. I sniffled back tears for the poor thing which suffered so much before it died. Orxlon was right, these beasts were savages. Nothing deserved a death as cruel as that. And seeing how fat they were, I wouldn't doubt they'd want to do the same to Orxlon or me, just to eat us.

When they had eaten and drank more of what I could only guess was alcohol of some sort, they quieted.

Soon, their snores reached me and the sun disappeared as it sank low in the sky, the moons coming up in its stead. I crawled out of the mudhole, the skies threatening another storm in the distance. Carefully crawling away from the enormous tree and in the opposite direction of the Dausers, I paused long enough to look back to be certain that no one had seen me or was coming after me. Satisfied they had not, I stood erect and shook my legs and arms from the stiffness and took off in a quiet run in the opposite direction of the beasts who lay sleeping.

When the path opened to an easier trail, I realized I had made it back to where I started earlier in the day. The clouds rolled in hiding the moons and thunder boomed in the distance. A moment later, the deluge poured, but I didn't mind. Mud and grime washed from my body and clothing. A giggle escaped my lips when I thought about the fat aliens I had left behind, as they laid all over the ground near the mud puddle tree. The river loomed ahead and tears of joy poured from my eyes. I just wanted to find Orxlon.

The rain let up as quickly as it came, and the clouds parted, allowing the moons to light my path. I walked along the river, following it downstream. Surely, I would stumble upon the cave soon. A gripping thought rang through my head as I jogged alongside the fast-flowing river. It flowed much faster than it had earlier before the rains hit. Flash floods often hit the jungles on Earth. Astavail probably had the same problem. What if the Dausers had discovered him after I left? What if they had captured him and made a game of torturing him before killing and eating him? My hand flew over my mouth to keep from screaming his name. If there were a Dauser in the area, they'd hear me.

That did it. With my mind made up, I marched ahead with resolve. If I ever saw Orxlon again, I would tell him that I have feelings for him. It's true that I had an attraction physically to him, but while in the mud hole watching the horrible things the Dausers did to that poor animal I realized my heart ached to see his bronzed face one more time. I yearned to feel his capable arms encircling me, protecting me and easing my worry and panic. No human ever did that for me, and yet this alien who was my genetic match did. Now if only I could find the cave and him.

Chapter 8

ORXLON

I stirred as the bright light danced over the cave when the sun hit the water. Stiff and sore from sleeping on the cave floor, I didn't care as long as I had my mate with me. We had survived the night. Rolling over, I saw nothing but the empty cave.

"Raven?" I called out softly. Tuning my ears outside the cave, I heard the morning songs of the creatures of Astavail, but no human.

The water sprayed me as I emerged and glanced around the falls for Raven and for the Dausers. Seeing neither, I clamored up the embankment to the top and scanned the area.

"Raven? Where are you?" I called out again without being so loud as to alert others of my presence.

What if she had left the cave for a drink of water, or to relieve herself and the Dausers had captured her? What if she had run away from me, hoping to escape to a vacation that did not exist? My heart sank at the thought as I scanned the land around the river. Footsteps led away, but disappeared just where the jungle met the water's edge.

I could see the appeal to traipse through the sparse trees, given a path for good footing. If she had come this way, she would have discovered, however, that it led nowhere. Unfortunately, my tracking abilities didn't serve me well in the overgrown jungle that surrounded the simple path. Raven could have gone in any direction. I'd stick with the footprints I had found and circle back to follow the river. What if she had wandered out and gotten lost? The question stabbed at my hearts. What if she ran away from me, even after our close moments the previous day?

Dragon's blood. I should have followed my original instinct to take her straight to my home world. She'd be safe now and not wandering the dense jungle of Astavail with the sick Dausers hot on her trail. I had to find her before they did, or else. My body shuddered at the thought. Such a beautiful creature she was, and she'd put up a fight which would entice them further to toy with her before devouring her. I could only hope that if they captured her, they'd cage her for auction. That would be the better fate, though neither one was ideal.

I didn't know what to do, so I followed the logical path where the footprints disappeared. Not too far through the sparse trees the Dausers had set up camp. It appeared Raven had wandered right into their midst. A pile of bones cleaned with their acid saliva and gnawed with their sharp rows of teeth sat beside a fire pit. Stepping out, I risked discovery, as they had wandered to the river not too far from their camp. Their thick voices traveled, a merry sound as they had enjoyed a feast the previous night. I plucked a larger bone and sniffed. *Rolqial.* The animal must have put up a fight worthy of their enjoyment. My hearts picked up, beating hard once again. They would look at Raven as a tasty feast as well if they found her. Or they would cage her and sell her at the Trianks Auction House in Sector 13F. I could not allow that. No cages sat among the other things at their camp. Their voices loomed closer, so I dove into the shadows and retreated slowly while listening to them speak.

"Cekfi caught the scent." The leader spoke to the group. Cekfi grinned, his fat jowls jiggled.

"Sure did. Followed it to the river. Must be something new to the planet," Cekfi replied.

My hair bristled. He couldn't be talking about me because they knew the Salzonis. They didn't know Terran, or at least not this group of Dausers, as far as I could tell. Raven wandered around out here, leaving her scent behind, enticing these savages to track and capture her. She played right into their game. I had to stop them. Something more than a fire diversion would be required. The sap trees had burned out. Perhaps they thought stray lightning had struck and ignited the small grove. It only pulled them away for a few moments.

They broke camp and prepared to track the new creature. I had to stay on their tail just in case they found Raven. I'd fight to my death to save her, whatever it took. Though my height and weight towered over the terrible creatures, they had great speed and agility despite the layers of blubber on their bodies. At least they'd stop at any water source to cool themselves once they took off.

The trail followed the river, the one called Cekfi leading the way. His nose jutted forward as he sniffed the air. When they stopped by the river for a dip, I took advantage and found avufca berries. The pungent fruit could mask scents and would easily stain with their bright red juice. Spreading the berries along the trail, just outside of their range, I covered it with undergrowth and stomped. The aroma reached my nose, causing me to gag from the odor. The Dausers would lounge in the river, bathing and eating before picking up and traveling once again. I fled upstream and covered all the trails I could find, masking anything they may have sniffed, covering Terran scent, I hoped.

The river flowed fast and heavy. Would Raven try to cross it? I somehow doubted it, knowing how she felt about getting wet at the cave. I could do the same on the other side, but the Dausers were drying and gathering their things, ready to hit the trail again. I had to be quick.

Ducking down into a ravine, I clamoured to the other side and up the hill. My comm had no signal deep inside the jungle. Once at the peak, I hid behind a small grove of trees and pulled up the comm. Bruns appeared in a hazy three-dimensional image that shimmered before me.

"Orxlon, where are you?" he asked.

"I'm not sure. Can you paint me here?"

"Yes, pulling up scanners and have you on dot. I see the Dausers as well. Where is Raven?" he asked.

"I don't know," I said as I growled. "She wandered off from our hiding spot. I'm not sure if she's lost or if she ran away from me. I need backup. Report on the ship," I commanded.

"We've lifted it from the ground. The hull cracked, and repairs are more intensive than we had hoped. Rescue is bringing the materials needed to fix it. Should be ready within a week of gathering the supplies," Bruns replied.

"Can you spare a few, well armed and ready to fight?" My fists flexed.

"If you need us, then yes," Bruns said.

Good answer. "Come to me. Keep me on your scanners since I can't tell you where I am. I fear the Dausers are tracking Raven. If they catch her, we must be ready to fight. I won't lose my mate," I told him.

"Have you claimed her then?"

Silence filtered in as I formed the words. "Not yet. I will," I replied. My firm resolve would prove successful. I could feel her defenses weakening while we were together inside the cave.

"We're on our way, sir," Bruns answered.

I kept the *Remis* on my scanner. The comm blinked, the image distorting as I hiked through the crags and valleys, but when I reached the tops of the hills, the signal came in clear. I had no choice but to keep up with both.

"If Raven comes back there, let me know," I said to the crew on my comm as I took a breather.

"Sir, Astavail has shifting magnetic poles. It switched directions while we were en route to you. Now you're not on our screen any longer. Can you see us?" Bruns spoke frantically.

My hearts dropped when I saw the blank scanner screen. Even the Dausers were no longer on my scanner, though I had them in my eyesight across the small valley. I kept more than enough distance between us so that they wouldn't catch my scent. I stayed downwind as much as possible, though that was becoming tricky as well.

Just as if nature decided to play a cruel trick, a storm began to blow in, the clouds dark and foreboding. No one traveled through these ravines as the lower levels of the jungle would flood during the heavy rains. I worried Raven could drown if she weren't in a safe location. Thunder boomed overhead as lightning flashed. I hunkered down under a small grove of trees, hoping a strike wouldn't catch any of them on fire. The storms of Astavail often lasted for hours, though in some cases they'd blow through within minutes. This one wasn't letting up, though, and neither the Dausers nor I were moving.

"Raven, where are you?" I asked quietly, though no one answered. The rock in the pit of my stomach ached as I wondered about her safety. For two days she'd been off my senses, her heart beating apart from mine.

"Sir, you have suddenly popped up on our scanners. Please stay where you are so we can catch up with you," Bruns said through my comm.

I peered across the ravine at the Dauser camp. They ambled around, ready to hunt or move on. "I can't promise that," I told him.

"If you move and the magnetic forces shift again, we could lose communication with you altogether," Bruns warned.

He was right. "I know. I can't risk losing the Dausers, though. If they find Raven…"

"I know you're concerned. We'll work together as a team to rescue her. Just hold on. We should reach you before the day is out," he promised.

"That's too long. I'm not waiting. Do what you can to map my location now. My only concern at the moment is Raven. No word from the ship about her?"

"No, sir. Nothing. I left orders to alert us the moment she shows," he said.

The Dausers moved not so much away as they did to the side. The land tore into lower levels where the scanner signal broke up. I could follow the Dausers, but then what if they found Raven. As only one Salzoni, I could not fight the lot alone. They would sacrifice both of us. If I waited for my crew, we'd stand a much better chance at beating them. But I stood a chance of losing sight of the Dausers and Raven altogether. They didn't have her yet, and that was in my favor.

I dug my heels in on the hilltop under the grove of trees. I would be in a much better position to fight the Dausers with my crew by my side.

"Bruns? I'm waiting for you. I may move sideways, to keep the enemy in my sight, but I'm not moving out of range," I said into the comm.

Chapter 9

The ground gave way as I followed the river downstream, hoping to find the cave and Orxlon again. My body fell with a splash into the river, the icy water swirling around me. I screeched, but the tumbling water hid my voice. No one heard, and I didn't want those dreaded aliens to know where I was. I'm an excellent swimmer, when on Earth, when in the right gear. My pants and top were saturated with water, but being lightweight helped. The shoes had traction and some heavy bits on the bottom that did not allow my legs to float. Do I pull them off and swim to shore only to be barefoot in the horrid jungle? Lost and barefoot was not exactly what I wanted. Wet, dingy shoes were better than bare feet. Being hungry for days, my weak body couldn't swim as fast as I needed to reach the shore. I kept my feet kicking, spending what little energy I had until I finally reached shallow water. The struggle to stand was better than the struggle to swim in full clothing. My teeth chattered as I waded to the shore and pulled my body out of the water. The storms had caused the river to race as its level increased.

I collapsed onto the ground, the rocks and grass not providing a very comfortable spot, but at least it was a little warmer in the sun as it peeked around the clouds. My shoes, which could have drowned me from their weight as I came across, came off easily as I laid back, allowing the rays of the strange yellow green light to bathe me, warm me, and dry me. I didn't care if anyone found me. I was too tired and hungry and cold. I needed warmth. I took in deep breaths as I peered up at the sky. At least I was out in the open, where I wouldn't go into a full-blown panic attack.

"Oh, Orxlon, where are you?" I cried quietly.

My stomach rolled with an angry growl. I hadn't had actual food in days, not since we crashed on this God-forsaken planet. Paradise, my ass. My eyes closed for what I thought would be just for a moment. I awoke some time later when I heard the jungle floor snapping behind me. Bolting upright, I shoved my feet into my now-dry shoes. I'd slept for a while. Another snap behind me and I jumped up and dove to the side, behind an outcropping of rocks at the river's edge where it hid me well. My parched mouth smacked, so I reached and scooped a handful of water. I spat, spewing the rancid water from my lips. It swirled with green and brown, like the algae ponds had uprooted and flowed by right at that moment.

Sickening gurgles resounded from the depths of my belly. I was hungry and thirsty and nothing around could stop the intensity of it. Swallowing with a dry mouth proved fruitless as I swayed with dizziness. I propelled forward while hoping to stumble upon the *Remis,* and kept going despite my physical weakness. I would not allow myself to perish in the wild of this horrible planet and at the mercy of the blood-thirsty aliens. I would not become game to their sickening desires. Shivers raced down my spine at the thought of what they'd do to me if I were caught.

Hot tears flooded my eyes. As much as Orxlon pissed me off by being so bullish, he would be a welcome sight right now. My heart ached to find him, to relax in his embrace. I should have known better. Perhaps Supernova Escapes was right, and he and I are a perfect match.

"*Oh!*" I leapt ahead as the cave, *our* cave, came into view. Coming up on the other side, I realized the ship would be behind me somewhere. Still, maybe, just maybe, Orxlon awaited me inside. I clamored down the embankment, memories of our first time finding the place flooding through my mind. Even though I had resisted him while inside the cave, a part of me felt safe. Why was I so hard-headed? I lamented wearing white shoes. My thoughts were on my appearance and my bags at the ship as well as the being that wanted nothing more than to protect me.

Water rushed over me and it didn't bother me much as I leapt through and thrust myself into the cave. It was empty, lonely, and yet familiar. Had he come back and found me gone? What if he had and then assumed that I had run away? I did, though. Stupid girl! My hands flailed to my head. What if he had left me here after giving up on me? If that were the case, then he's not my destined soulmate after all. What if he's out there, though, looking for me? I had no way of knowing.

"Orxlon, where are you?" I asked, my voice echoing

through the small cave.

Resolve settled inside my heart. I had to get back to the ship. His crew could alert him then that I was safe with them. At least the ship would still be on the planet after crashing. They said it would take a couple of weeks to repair it. How long had it been? I had lost track of the days. The days on this planet are short and I feel as if the planet is playing games with my mind.

After inhaling deeply, I pushed through the water again, set on traipsing back to the ship. Instead, a net landed over me, and someone grabbed me, pulling me away.

"No!"

The fat blubbery aliens looked into my face, smug and ready to haul me off to my doom. I cried and tried to break loose. Why were they so quick and yet so fat? It made no sense. I stumbled along over the rocks, my foot slipping, and nearly tumbled into the stream. Better that and drown than the fate that awaited me in their hands.

Fight or flight was something I never really quite understood until this moment. Even when the *Remis* crashed I still had no clue about it. My body flooded with strength, surprising me. The creatures laughed as I struggled, but somehow I broke loose. Turning back, I jumped into the rocky water below. It would be better to allow the stream to carry me away than to let these horrid creatures take me to their camp.

The fat one that had me in his grasp for a moment yelled out a sharp gurgling sound that pierced my ears. Through too many rocks and not enough water, I clamored to the middle of the stream, half running and half slipping, because the rocks had a thin layer of slick algae atop them, causing me to constantly lose footing. I crashed into a rock, my feet sliding into the water. The creatures jumped into the stream effortlessly. *No!* I flung my body forward, trying to outrun the beasts, but they proved faster on the slippery rocks and water that I. Perhaps I might have escaped if I had taken off on the ground rather than in the stream. My efforts thwarted, their fat hands grabbed me, two more securing me tightly. I had lost.

I became resigned to my fate, realizing the Dausers far outpowered me. My mouth tried swallowing. I desperately needed water and food. Yet, I had the feeling that I was about to become the meal. Looking to the side, I spied a pair of eyes in the dense brush. It was a friendly face, and a finger that came to rest upon his lips. The universal sign of *be quiet.* My heart soared, my pulse quickened and calmed all within the same moment. A mixture of complete gratitude and something else surfaced. *Love?* Did I feel love for the alien? A smile stretched over my face, only for a moment, as I realized everything would be okay.

The Dausers held little hiding spots in their disorganized camps. I sat upon a stump, my hands bound behind me, while they scurried about, doing things that I didn't understand. Their grunts and gurgles I could not decipher. Looking around, I kept an eye out for Orxlon. He had a plan, surely. He had nodded at me, as if to plead with me to be patient.

The Dauser that had pulled me through the jungle

came to me and grunted. I shook my head.

"I'm sorry, I can't understand you. Can you understand me?"

He grew frustrated, pursed his lips and walked away. Another came back with a container of water and a spout on the end. I nodded and opened my mouth. Yes, your meal needs to be refreshed before you partake of her. They stepped to me and lifted the container as the water poured forth, too quickly for me to drink very well, but much of it landed inside my mouth. I slurped thirstily, jutting my tongue forward, probably looking like an animal. Perhaps they didn't understand how to place it at my mouth, but then again they probably didn't have a clue as to what I was.

Once the water filled my belly, I felt better as I sat on the stump. My hands behind my back were of little help, though I worked the bindings. The waxy cords loosened easily, but I kept them inside my hands so as to not alert them to the state of my bonds. I would let them think that they had me bound tightly and unable to run. Funny enough, they didn't tie me to the stump. Someone had their keen eyes on me all the time, thought, so running would be pointless. I waited, knowing Orxlon worked on some plan to rescue me. Somehow the thought of a reunion with him made me warm inside. The alien bought me as his Terran mail order bride, even though it was in the form of a ruse to get me to show up for a vacation that didn't exist. The thought of seeing his body naked excited me. The package he carried surely outshined any human male I had ever seen. How could I deny the way he made me feel? It was as if my life belonged in his hands. This was an odd comfort that settled into my very soul. Even in the dark, dank cave, he had comforted me in a way that I thought impossible. A smile stayed on my face. These beings didn't know that I was smiling. Their fat blubbery faces didn't show emotions, or at least nothing that I recognized. No, I relaxed and waited. Orxlon had a plan. He'd come for me. I'd submit to him if he pulled it off. I'd be his, because I wanted it. That fate sounded so much better than the current situation of being dinner for the fat ones.

Chapter 10

At least she's okay. Her smile made my three hearts beat in unison once again, and I knew then that everything would be alright. I just needed to figure out a way to rescue Raven. The Dausers hadn't discovered my presence, which gave me the edge. Their plans for my mate remained unclear. They spoke of naming the new creature they found, which I'm assuming is her. At least they have said nothing about eating her. Maybe she's a curiosity, one that would keep her alive until they tired of her.

Poor dear, her tongue came out and lapped up the water they so carelessly poured over her face. Thirst became obvious to me as well, but the river tainted with the fresh storms. I'm sure Raven discovered the stench in the water and avoided drinking it. At least Supernova gave me an intelligent mate.

"Tarkatartar," the leader said and nodded toward Raven.

My spine prickled. The word meant *pleasure bearing.* They had no intentions of eating her, but intended to use her for their pleasure. My mortal enemy wanted to taint and rape my mate, and I could not allow that to happen. Raven perched on the stump, her eyes scanning the area, no doubt searching for me. Her hands tied behind her moved for a while and finally stopped. A small smile formed on her lips and I realized she must have undone the bindings. *Good girl!* This would make it easier to rescue her before they had the chance to do unspeakable things to her precious body.

I moved around, trying to find an opening when they would be preoccupied with something else. Unfortunately, someone constantly kept vigil over her. Another diversion might draw their attention away, but I doubt they'd run for a fire again. The sap trees were fewer here in the dense jungle than closer to the edge.

"Can you paint my location?" I asked into the comm.

Bruns face came in. "Sir, we have you again. What's the status?"

"They have Raven. She's safe for now, but they are talking of defacing her. I will not allow that. I'm outnumbered, so I need you here soon," I replied.

"We are on the way, about two leagues out. We have the Dauser camp on screen. Many have fanned out from their camp," he informed me.

Smart savages. Keep extras hidden in case she tried to escape. "Okay, I see none very close to where I'm hiding. Come to me; we'll grab her and run," I told him.

If a fight ensued, I had a better chance with my crew around me.

"Yes, Captain. We're heading there now," Bruns said.

The waver in the magnetic field caused him to go off screen suddenly. I hoped they had mapped the general direction and would make it to me before the enemies took Raven away. I'd have to jump in and try to save her on my own if that were the case. It would prove futile, though, because they'd overpower me and then they'd have their way with her and kill me. No, I needed to wait and hope that they'd do nothing with her.

"Sir, please step toward us," Bruns requested through my comm.

I left my hiding place and rushed back into the bush to find my crew. Instead, I nearly lost my way as the comm drew blank again. The damned magnetic field caused too many disturbances in the scanner.

The jungle looked the same in every direction. Being disoriented didn't help as I stumbled around, trying to contact my crew. My finger pounded the blank screen on the comm, the distorted images giving me no sign of their whereabouts.

I had been too careless, the opening not hiding me as I stepped out in hopes of a better signal. The *Remis* had to be close; the signal bouncing from it should help. A crackle behind me caused me to lurch into the dense jungle too late. The capture net landed over my head and clung to my body. Hot putrid breath hit the back of my neck as I turned and came face to face with a Dauser.

"Prize." He breathed, his teeth crooked and angled from gnawing on too many bones.

"No," I growled as I struggled. If it were just the one, I could beat him, but with the net over me and three upon me, they outnumbered and overpowered me easily. I had to fight, I had to give it my all. Maybe my crew would find their camp and save Raven, if not me. At least, they could carry her to safety. My hearts ached at the thought of losing my life before I lived with her as my mate. Struggling only caused the net to stick to me more, so I stopped. Carefully, I lifted it until I nearly had it to my head. The fat grunting crag pulled the net tightly, closing it around my throat. My arms stuck to my side, unable to free myself.

"No, he's part of the sacrifice. The gods will be happy," another said.

Happy? Gods? Oh no! Not only did they enjoy playing with their food, they sacrificed live animals to their gods to gain favor. I had to remain calm to free myself and save the one with whom I'm destined. She didn't deserve this. I'd sacrifice myself for her.

"Stop. Take me, sacrifice me, but let the female go. I won't fight," I told them.

They stopped and glared at me, as if I spoke rubbish. I knew a little of their language. "Please."

"No. Two better than one. She's our special sacrifice," he replied.

"You touch her, I'll have your head," I screamed back at him.

He grinned and a sick chuckle spewed from his lips along with long strings of slimy saliva. "I think you have it wrong. We'll have your head. Tasty Salzonian brains for our next meal," he said. The others laughed with him as they pulled me along.

When we entered the camp, I saw with great horror the stump upon which Raven had sat, now empty. Had they already done horrible things to her? I turned, ripping through the netting, struggling and fighting with every bit of strength I had. Enraged, I came at them, my teeth bearing and growling.

They hooted all the more as they shoved me along and thrust me into the animal skin shelter. I was flung to the floor, the netting still sticking to me.

"Orxlon, oh god, are you okay?" Raven rushed toward me. My eyes looked up at her.

"Are you alright? Did they hurt you?"

"No, they threw me in here after discovering I had untied my binds," Raven replied as she helped pull the net from my body.

"We can escape," I said, my voice barely audible.

"No, this place is sewn tightly, and they posted a guard or two outside the only door," she said as she held out her hands.

"It's okay," I said. She thrust herself into my arms, her small body clinging to mine. With her by my side, I could face anything. My hearts settled into a rhythm, her small human heart thumping in unison with mine.

"I thought I'd never see you again. I'm so sorry," she said as she pulled back. Large tears flooded her eyes.

"What happened? When I awoke, you were gone. So many thoughts have been in my head about it," I said as I shook my head.

Her hand came up and wiped across her nose as she sniffed. "Okay, I admit it, I wanted to go back to the ship because I wasn't sure about what you were doing. But then, I got turned around, and I saw these dreadful beasts. I hid in a mud puddle, but the rains kept coming. Eventually, I escaped and found the river. Then I found the cave again. Orxlon, I had somehow crossed the river again after crossing once before and don't even remember doing it. I don't know why I thought you'd be in the cave, but you weren't. Oh no, so much has happened. I missed you so. I came out and they—they grabbed me. Then I thought my life was over. Oh, did I tell you I saw them eat an animal? They are horrible, horrible beings. They toyed with it, tortured it and then killed and ate it," she cried. Raven's words came out fast as pent-up anger and fear bubbled inside me.

My hands stroked her hair as I held her closely and listened. Finally, she paused, her bloodshot eyes peering into mine.

"I must look a mess," she said as she sniffled.

"Oh, my lovely Terran. You look like my beautiful mate. I'm so sorry this has happened to you," I replied.

"It's my fault. I ran away from you. But then again I didn't *want* to run away from you. I wanted to find you again, but I couldn't," she said. Her body shuddered in my embrace.

The fat one opened the door and glared at us. "Stop that. Sacrifice must be in good shape. The fires are hot, you will make happy our god," he said before turning and leaving again.

"What?" Raven shook her head. She didn't understand a word the savage uttered.

"It's okay, help is on the way. Nevermind them," I told her. I didn't want to alarm her with unnecessary fear. I had enough fear for both of us. They would soon tie us together and burn the fire hot to roast us both. After that, they'd feast upon our carcasses.

"What did he say, Orxlon? Tell me."

Oh, her eyes pierced my soul as she stared at me. I wanted nothing to come between us, so honesty with

Raven would be required.

"He said you and I are their sacrifice," I told her softly.

She nodded and grew unbelievably calm. "I knew it. I saw how they treated that poor creature. They want to eat everything in their path," she replied stoically.

"Especially a Salzonian," I added with a chuckle. Why not laugh? I glanced at my comm. A signal came up that let me know that my crew were nearby. This gave me a renewed hope that we'd soon escape.

"That's horrible," she laughed with me.

"My crew is nearby. They know where we are," I said as I pointed to my comm. "I'm sure they are trying to figure out the best way to save us."

"Try to talk to them," she encouraged.

I pulled up the image which flickered in and out, grainy and hissing.

"What's going on in there?" growled the guard at the door.

"Help us, now. They want to burn us alive," I said, hoping my crew heard me over the hissing.

I quickly hid the comm when the grunt opened the door. He grinned, his row of rotten teeth showing and a putrid breath blowing toward us. "It won't be long. The fire's hot and ready for the sacrifice," he announced.

Chapter 11

I clung to Orxlon. He calmed me in a way that I couldn't understand. Perhaps that's why Supernova Escapes called me his *perfect* mate, because we had a chemistry that went beyond comprehension. The journey started so differently before we were captured. I had carefully packed my bag with matching shoes and even jewelry. I don't know what I expected. An alien that appreciated my fine tastes in fashion? Now that seemed so trivial. Just surviving and believing I had a future took every ounce of optimism I could muster.

"Where is your crew?" I asked.

"Don't worry, they will arrive just in time," Orxlon said as he grinned. Though his handsome ruddy face presented me with a smile, it didn't reach his eyes. It was as if he didn't really believe his own words. I didn't press him on it, either. It was better for us to believe that we had a chance than to fall prey to the horrors the Dausers wanted to perform on us.

"Orxlon, I need to come clean about something," I said as I fidgeted with the edge of my outfit.

"What's that?" he asked.

"I know you held me under false pretenses when we first met. I mean, I thought I was on the way to a vacation. But you came to claim me. Neither of us were fair with our reactions. I didn't like how mean you were with your crew and with me, but I see how these Dausers are and realize that you would never harm your crew," I admitted.

He flinched. "I'm the captain of the ship. Admittedly, Salzonians aren't the nicest creatures out there. We esteem ourselves better than some. My crew came onboard willingly, even the Baedelions. They work a year at a time, serving the captain, and in return, I deliver them back to their home planet with good pay. It's been this way for centuries. They know that if I hire them, they become part of my crew, and I treat them like a Salzonian Captain treats his crew," he added.

I blinked. I mean, sure, he makes sense. Still, couldn't he have been nicer to them? Always barking orders, demanding things. He even did it with me, lest I forget. Yet, I stood there with him, his presence calming me, my heart beating with a different rhythm. One that made my cheeks blush rosy.

"Okay, that took me a little by suprise. But I need to admit something to you."

"Yes?" His bushy brow lifted, his bronze muscles flexing.

"I admit that I have feelings for you," I told him.

"What does that mean, exactly?" Orxlon asked.

I laughed. "Right, you're not accustomed to Terran terms. I like you. I guess I like you more than I care to admit."

Just then the door opened, and the blob grabbed me, pulling me toward the opening. *"No! Orxlon,"* I cried out.

"Don't fight. Don't give them a reason to harm you," he told me as they pulled me away from the tent.

The creature thrust me into a square container that stood with water. A bathtub, perhaps? The creep uttered something guttural at me and shoved me further into it. I made a splash and fell onto one knee.

Orxlon howled. The creep turned and walked a few steps away to see what the commotion was about. I didn't think twice; I leapt out of the tub and took off in a dead run for the jungle. The dense gnarled branches nearly stopped me, but I kept running, breaking into the trees while being jabbed by branches and jumping over the small shrubs on the jungle floor.

I ran, but not fast enough. The beasts came up behind me quickly and caught hold of my hair. I yelled.

"Ouch! *Stop!* Orxlon, *help!*" I screamed.

The beast grunted and pulled me back toward the camp as we stumbled through the thick mass of trees. How I ran as far as I did, I didn't know. Perplexed by the speed of the fat pieces of shit, I cried as he shoved me near a raging fire. Two more stood beside me, towering over my small body. The one that caught me held my hands at my back. I realized too late how I had played right into their hands. They enjoyed the game of chasing their prey. Oh no. I would be their meal soon.

Orxlon came out of the tent. They had bound his hands behind him and two more escorted him until he stood in front of me. Utter sorrow creased his face as he looked at me. Neither of us could do anything to save ourselves.

The fat leader stood before me with grunts and gurgles pouring from his mouth, his beady eyes set upon mine. He prattled on about something, Orxlon's face skewing into horror. He struggled to get loose, but the two with him pulled the binds even tighter. The beast kept uttering at me, but I couldn't understand him. He turned angrily and shouted at Orxlon.

"He says you are to know, he's not killing me." Orxlon's face skewed in sorrow.

"What? That's great!" Tears stung my eyes.

"No, he wants me to live while I watch my mate being burned alive. Raven, I'm so sorry that I failed you. I thought my crew would have been here by now. I will join you in the afterlife. I will get away somehow. I can't live without you, not now that I've found you," he lamented.

Sorrow gripped me hard, my body shaking from uncontrollable shivers. "Orxlon, don't blame yourself. My parents died on another planet, so it only seems fitting that I will too. I will join them soon. Please promise me that you will survive and get away from them. Punish them and look for another mate to replace me. I'm not worth dying for," I told him.

"Oh, but you are. Little Terran, you have no clue. Inside my chest beats three hearts, that up until I met you beat out of sync. I can feel your heartbeat when you're nearby. I sense your moods. There is no other mate for me," he promised.

His words hit me like hailstones falling from an angry sky. I yelled as I struggled, trying to free myself from the damn savages. "Let me go!" I screamed.

The beasts grunted and their hands bore into me. One approached and tied my hands to the wood, splinters dug deep into my inner arms, piercing my skin. I didn't care. I looked at Orxlon. I would focus on him until my life left my body. It was too late now that I had realized how much I cared for him. If only I had trusted him before.

"Orxlon, I love you. I would have surrendered to you, allowing you to claim me as your forever mate," I said tearfully.

"No!" he screamed.

Tears flowed hard from my eyes as my nose ran with its own liquid. I didn't care. In a matter of moments I'd be burning. "Goodbye, Orxlon," I said to my love.

He watched in horror as they tightened the bindings around my wrists and to the pole. My arms curved unnaturally behind me. Two Dausers moved toward the raging fire with giant shovels, digging into the embers at the bottom, and plucking up a burning bit of wood.

One last glance at Orxlon, I squeezed my eyes shut. Please let it be fast. I don't deal well with pain. A collective gasp followed by incredible zaps and cries startled me as my eyes popped open. All around me the ground turned into Dausers fighting Salzonians. Someone untied Orxlon, and a Dauser jumped at him, sword drawn. I screeched, fear gripping me as I watched the one I loved fight for his life. A warrior by trade, Orxlon grabbed the fat Dauser and wrapped his powerful arms around his neck. The same arms that embraced me and calmed me took the life of his mortal enemy.

To my right, a Dauser sliced through one of the crew

members. Orxlon's face grimaced as Sucin crumpled to the ground. With a swift cry of war, he launched at the one with a Dauser sword in his hand. Delivering the death blow with the very weapons with which the enemy tried killing his crew, Orxlon shoved it through him, pinning the beast to the ground. I looked away. Blue black blood poured around the sword. Orxlon jumped over him and grabbed a laser blaster, making quick work of it. Several Dausers ran into the jungle as Salzonians took off in pursuit.

Suddenly, a Dauser sliced through the ropes tying me to the wooden pole. He grabbed my shoulder, yanking hard and pulling me toward the jungle. I screeched again and turned, kicking with all I had. The futile attempts did little to stop the beast as he pulled me along. Still, I gave it my all. Where was Orxlon? A quick scan of my eyes through the bloody battle told me that Orxlon had a Dauser on him, his great arms wrapped around his neck.

"No! Orxlon! No!" I screamed. Struggling, I tried to cut loose from the maniac, but he proved stronger than me, holding me to him. His fat arm wrapped around my neck in the same way Orxlon had taken the life of a Dauser. Air caught in my lungs and my cheeks burned. No! I didn't want to die like this. Somehow burning at the stake felt like a better death. I squeezed my eyes shut. If I ever make it out of this alive, I will pledge my life to Orxlon. Tears clouded my vision, even while being choked. I grew quiet. The Dauser sensed my giving up and loosened his grip just enough that I let out the air and gulped in another. Playing dead had its advantages. Yes, that was the key to my survival.

Orxlon disappeared from my vision. Blood splattered over the ground, the cries and groans of the injured and dying drowned the otherwise chirpy, wailing noise of the jungle. War cries filled the air around me. Was it Orxlon and his crew? Was it the Dausers? Perhaps the arm around my neck grew tighter, and I hadn't realized it. Suddenly, everything grew quiet except for a nice hissing in my ears, a welcome reprieve. No struggle, no fight, just sweet oblivion. Darkness encompassed me. Someone yelled my name. Orxlon? Did he survive? No matter, my body relaxed and the hissing calmed. It was nothing but a dream in which I was walking along a beautiful path in a different wood. Orxlon was by my side, showing me his world which was far more beautiful than I could have ever imagined. Above us, a ringed planet rose along with the small moon, the rosy sky glowing with the orange and yellows of the strange planet.

Chapter 12

The Dauser laid at my feet, dead. He had tried choking Raven and she passed out, but was still breathing. My three hearts thumped in unison as I could feel her heart beating strongly. I watched in horror as she lost consciousness, but right before she stopped struggling. If Raven died I would choke every one of the enemy in sheer rage. Our connection proved strong and was the only reason I didn't rush toward her, because I knew her heart had continued beating. I had to kill every single Dauser to avenge the grief they had brought upon my mate.

The fat beast slumped toward the ground. I had choked three so far. Every time I looked at Sucin lying on Astavail dead, my body shook with rage. Gars pitched a laser blaster to me. He stepped back and drew his sword before taking off after the Dauser that had just killed his brother. I turned, seeing my crew embattled with the scum. Carefully aiming, I pulled the trigger and the deathblow lasers had flown, hitting the targets where it counted. Stripes formed across the backs of their heads and on their faces. I wasn't toying with them. I was aiming to kill. Satisfied Raven would be fine, I took off after the three who disappeared into the jungle. Tirx and Al'vo trailed behind me, pursuing the enemy to the bitter end. The Dausers may be fat, but their feet carried them faster than a Salzonian could run. It didn't matter, though. We'd run after them until they fell over from exhaustion. They may have speed over us, but we have endurance over them. Their fat bodies were fast, but they became tired quickly. I drew my sword, enjoying the sensation of the blade sinking into the flesh of the enemy. A satisfaction that emerged from deep within me.

Suddenly, one of my hearts skipped out of beat. Raven! Spinning, I ran back to the camp and couldn't find her.

"Where's Raven?" I boomed.

Bruns stopped, the bloody sword in his hand as he gazed in the opposite direction.

"They must have grabbed her. There," he said and pointed.

No! A trail of blood as well as of dragging feet led into the deep jungle, where no path would aid me in pursuit. They had her again and they were running. My hearts thumped wildly out of sync. My mate had disappeared too far for me to feel her. Panic set in as I took off in a dead run, my sword drawn as I sliced through the gnarled wood, leaving a path behind me. Keen eyes spotted the way, her body still unconscious as they drug her along. They wouldn't hold out for very long.

I injured one of them. The trail of blue-black blood spotted the way, dotted on leaves, the ground, and branches. A wicked smile stretched across my face, because I had them. My precious mate lived, her heartbeat now entering my senses again. My hearts boomed separately still, though, because of the fear Raven felt. She must be awake now, but unable to fight her captors

"Hold on, sweet Raven, I'm coming for you," I yelled out. My teeth ground together, the muscles in my jaw flexing and aching from doing so.

"Here, Orxlon," Frean said. He motioned ahead. The small being was loyal and faithful. Perhaps Raven was right. I should treat them as equals and not as inferior beings. They were risking their lives for her as much as I was.

I motioned for him to go around. We'd flank the scum, taking them by surprise. Suddenly, the path grew cold, the blue-black blood disappeared. The grunt stopped bleeding. The gnarled wood twisted around, impossible to move ahead. My hearts pounded separately as I no longer sensed Raven's presence. We must have headed in the wrong direction from them.

"Bruns, I'm in pursuit of Raven. Please send who you can my way," I said into the comm.

"Sir, the scanner doesn't work. We can't see you on our screens."

I peered at Frean. "Go back until you can reach Bruns. Lead them back to me. Paint the trail as you go. I will advance straight that way," I said as I motioned my hand.

Frean peered at the sky and nodded, I'm sure noting the position of the sun overhead before he disappeared. The damn lack of proper magnetic fields caused me to curse the decision to land on this planet, knowing it held volatile magnetic resonance.

It took forever. The jungle grew eerily quiet of anything other than the sounds of small critters. I gulped as icy fear grabbed hold of me. What if they had killed Raven? It would also explain why I couldn't feel her presence any longer.

"Raven." My mind played tricks on me. I saw her peek out from behind a tree as if nothing was wrong. Her sweet smile invited me to join her. Impulsively. I stepped toward her, ready to take the plunge to be with her. I frowned as I shook my head. No. I couldn't lose her, not now. I had traveled across the galaxy to be with her. I had risked everything to claim my one true mate. I would not let her go so easily. Where were they? Where was Frean? Why couldn't I hear anything? My comm drew a blank, just a white screen hissing for the lack of a good signal.

Sheer instincts propelled me forward. I couldn't wait another second. Following my hearts' lead I took off leaving my crew behind. Finding Raven became my sole purpose. It wasn't long before my hearts tuned in unison once more. She was nearby. I kept going, my hearts beating stronger and faster. She was very close.

Her strained scream sounded to my right. "I'm coming, Raven," I said under my breath. Just ahead, three Dausers had slowed. Their mouths opened as they gulped air. I carefully pulled up the laser blaster. Three strikes would render them useless. Raven spotted me, her eyes growing large. I pulled my finger to my mouth and revealed the blaster. She nodded as I held up my hand, palm down. Two grunts had hold of her, but she wiggled enough as she lowered her body, her knees buckling. They released her to the ground and gave her a swift kick.

Snap. The first laser blast hit its target. The fat Dauser joined her on his knees, the life knocked out of him. Before the other two could react, I squeezed the trigger hitting the second. By then, the third looked around, its eyes swinging in my direction. I painted the target square between its eyes and squeezed. The creature flopped forward, dead.

Raven cried as she stumbled out of their midst. My arms opened as she threw herself at me, fully pressing her sweet, soft body into mine. I grabbed her to me and pulled her to a thicket nearby that I felt hid us well. She cried, burying her face into my chest. Leaning in, I took in her scent, her soft hair, and her heart being in rhythm with mine.

"Come, we need to get out of here," I told her.

She silently nodded and followed, her hand holding tightly to mine. We ran into Frean along the way.

"Oh sir, the others…"

"Let's go. We're all heading back to the ship."

We met the others along the way. Sorrow filled our journey back as we carried Sucin to give him a proper Salzonian space burial. Our faces drooped with sorrow as we approached the *Remis*. Help arrived at the ship while we were out, and no enemy had discovered the location. Applying nanobots to the hull helped to move the repairs along, and the ship soon looked brand new.

After we boarded and tested the engines, we launched, leaving Astavail behind, hoping never to land on the planet again. When the *Remis* safely reached hyper-speed, I checked on Raven. She'd hungrily ate and drank and had a long shower. I allowed her to use the facilities in my room since it offered a private shower and waste closet.

Lovely music hit my ears when I walked into my room. The shower ran, water splashing, and Raven sang. Her beautiful voice carried into my quarters, thrilling me beyond anything I could imagine. The sound of happiness, hope, and love filled my ears. I relaxed on my bunk after removing my boots. I planned on showering once Raven emerged. She continued with her sweet singing when the door thrust opened. She rubbed a towel through her wet hair, her body covered in a simple shirt and nothing else. Instantly, my members throbbed, her raw clean scent enticing me.

"Oh!" She stopped short as she looked up and saw me. I smiled, my brow lifting as I gazed over her nearly naked form.

She tore the towel from her hair and shoved it against her body. "I'm sorry! I thought I was alone. When you said I could use your room, I thought you'd stay away," she said, her eyes big.

"It is my room. And I came in here to check on you," I replied as I rolled toward her.

"And thought you'd make yourself comfortable. You heard me in the shower, no?"

I chuckled. "Sweet one, I did. Come, relax with me," I said as I patted the bed beside me.

Timidly, she approached, her eyes gazing over my body much like I did hers. With great ease, she crawled onto the bed and relaxed beside me, drawing her legs up and resting her arm on my chest. I kept smiling and kissed the top of her head as Raven sighed contentedly.

"Are you alright?"

"Mmm-hmmm." Lifting her chin, she gazed into my eyes shyly. "Are you? I'm so sorry about Sucin."

I squeezed my arms around her, stroking her wet hair. "Yes, that was bad. The Dausers are our mortal enemy. They don't think twice about killing us," I told her.

"I realized that when I saw them kill that hog-looking creature," she said as she shivered.

"I told you, they are ruthless. They have no regard for life."

"I am so overwhelmed," she told me, tears appearing in her eyes. I smiled wistfully at her, feeling the urge to kiss her sweet lips.

"Can I kiss you?"

Raven smiled. "I would like that."

Leaning in, she didn't fight me. My lips brushed against hers. Sweet, conforming, her seam parted and her tongue became pliable. I delighted in her flavor as my lips moved over hers. She groaned, not from duress, but from a sense of pleasure. The frenzy in my hearts pumped wildly in unison, thumping hard. My body ached to claim her, to take her. But I didn't need to pounce upon her. I needed a change and a shower. *Be gentle, Orxlon.* I kissed her neck, my hands exploring her body. She yawned and I cradled her as I scooted over to give her room as she nuzzled into my side and fell asleep.

Chapter 13

RAVEN

Could it be possible that I had found my purpose in life? Stirring, I stretched and yawned. Orxlon held me tightly all night. When I rolled over on his small bunk, I found the indention in his pillow but not him. Lifting from my slumber, I heard the shower running and a deep voice humming. An alien tune, probably something Salzonian. Orxlon had gotten up without disturbing me.

My legs swung over the edge of the bed. The water stopped running, and I looked at my bags sitting near a table on the other side of the small room. I should dress and appear modestly before him instead of taunting him with my body like I did all night. Out of his kindness, he had let me sleep after we kissed. I dreamed of muscular arms around me, making me so happy to be alive.

The door opened soon and he advanced. His naked body shone brightly before me. I averted my eyes as a fierce blush rode across my cheeks. I couldn't help but notice his cock as well as the smaller one, no doubt there to stimulate ovulation in female Salzonians. Instantly, it rose, standing out long and firm.

"Um, *Orxlon!* Let me leave so that you can dress," I

told him. He stopped, saying nothing. When I stood and approached the door, his dominant hand reached out and grabbed me. I didn't fight him. I turned, trembling as I beheld the intricate design on his chest. He grabbed my hand and placed it in the center.

"Feel that?" he asked.

I nodded, my eyes scanning over his impossible muscles.

"Three hearts beating as one. In a Salzonian male, the only time that happens is when he meets his one true mate. When I laid eyes upon you, my hearts began to beat in sync for the first time. That's how strongly I felt that you were for me, my mate," he told me.

"It's hard to comprehend this. Aren't there females on your home planet?"

"There is one female for every four males. We had a horrible pandemic years ago that killed most of the females. By the time they discovered a cure, it was too late. Evolution dictated fewer females being born. The generation before mine started looking outside our race for mates. Supernova Escapes came to us, offering a solution and a guaranteed genetic match. I traveled with a band of pirates before that," Orxlon told me as he lowered his head and shook it. "I'm not proud of that. I did it to forget having a mate. We looted crashed space ships and sold the goods to shady dealers around the system. It was not a good thing and I grew tired of it. I longed for a mate, someone with whom to build a family. I couldn't control the urges to do this. Raven, I played along with the ruse. Supernova Escapes said it would be best to meet you in a natural setting and to allow you a chance to fall in love with me. But I trust my fate to no one, so I took matters into my own hands. The agency agreed to my tactics. I paid them well for their services."

"I know. You went to great lengths to meet me. You more than proved your loyalty by rescuing me not once, but twice," I replied. We laughed, the moment charged with sexual energy. I couldn't help but notice his body and his members. "And this?" I peered down at the obvious elephant in the room.

He grinned. "Yes, I researched human anatomy. Supernova Escapes doesn't disappoint. This one requires stimulation in order for this one to work. On the females, it works to pleasure her, to stimulate her to ovulate, and in return, it prompts this one to fulfil the duty and plant our seed," Orxlon said so matter-of-a-factly.

I giggled. "Well, I'm not sure about making a baby, but I am curious how it works," I answered.

"Let me show you," Orxlon said. He leaned in, his lips finding mine as I encircled my arms around his neck. He lifted me and carried me to his bunk. I crawled to the pillows and lifted the thin shirt from my body. He beamed at me, his eyes taking in my nakedness.

"These are nice," he said as he cupped my breasts. "Mammaries are luscious and full of life." I giggled as he bent down, his lips brushing over a nipple that instantly stiffened. His gigantic hands rubbed down my body until he found the space between my legs. I moaned as he lifted and watched my face. His hand came up to his nose, and he sniffed.

"Ew, why?"

"I love the way you smell. This ignites my pleasure," he said as he lifted and showed me his raging double hardons.

"That's so cool," I said as I reached out and touched one of them. He moaned as my fingers rubbed over the tip of the smaller one. It vibrated inside my fingers. "Wow."

"Raven, I want to claim you as my mate. Once I do, you're mine for life. I will fight anyone who tries to come between us," he told me.

"You already have. Fought, that is," I said as I smiled.

"Yes, but I will not stand for losing you," he replied.

I shook my head. "Orxlon, I don't know. I want to, but this is heavy stuff. Like having sex with you is a marriage ceremony, binding me to you forever."

His hands trembled as he hovered over me. "Say the word and I will leave you now."

I said nothing as I looked into his eyes. He nodded and moved away from me. I grabbed his hand and shook my head. "No, don't leave. Stay. The answer is yes." The words fell from my lips, surprising me. It's as if my body took over. I opened my arms and pulled him to me.

Orxlon hovered, not fully leaning into me with his full weight. Our lips met, his mouth parting and his tongue finding mine. I lifted a leg around his waist, inviting him closer. I wanted him. My body ached with desire. He straightened, his hands roaming over my chest, squeezing my breasts, moving to the spot between my legs. With his cock in his hand, he leaned in. I moved until I met him, his body sliding over mine, our skin sliding against the other. He slowly, methodically penetrated through my tight hole, stretching me, filling me. There was no pain, just fullness and pleasure. The smaller member sawed against my spot as I swelled with desire, moving my body in unison with his. Orxlon moved slowly, gently, until he couldn't control himself any longer. He held onto my hip with one hand and slid to the floor. Standing, he took hold of my feet and placed them on his chest.

"Better control. I don't want to hurt you," he said breathlessly.

Magic sprouted as he pumped into me, his largest member moving in and out of me as the smaller of the two glided along my nub above. My back arched beneath him, my body trembling as pleasure built until I could no longer hold back.

"Oh! Yes!" I ground into him and into the bed as I came, crying in ecstasy. Never had I felt such heights of pleasure. He wildly pounded into me, no longer able to hold himself back.

"I'm making you mine, Raven. Little Terran, you are my mate. *I claim you!*" He lurched forward, his larger cock filling me, the hot liquid squirting as he moaned and thrust. His face skewed in a powerful orgasm. We rode the last wave together, our bodies in complete tune with the other. Finally, he finished and stumbled back from me. My legs quivered as I brought them to the edge of the bed. I swayed dizzily as I sat up, wishing I could keep experiencing Orxlon.

"Please, don't stop," I begged him.

He crawled onto the bed, his face still showing ecstasy as he drew me to him. Our kisses took on a fervor, one that wouldn't douse easily. I needed him again. I wanted him again. He flipped me until my back was at his front. His gigantic cock stayed erect as he took me from behind. His smaller member reached my sweet spot, causing the pleasure to ride over me again.

His arms encircled me afterward, our bodies lethargic from the powerful lovemaking and our hearts happy. The pain from losing my parents grew less intense as I found my purpose. I didn't like Supernova Escape's way of doing things, but it didn't matter any longer. I smiled and lifted to look Orxlon in his golden eyes.

"You told me that normally Supernova Escapes wants the *brides* to meet their alien mates in a natural setting, so that they fall in love?"

He chuckled. "Yes. And yes, I did it all wrong. I told you that I'm not patient, and I wanted to make sure I got my money's worth in my bride."

"And did you?"

"Oh, sweet one. You make the suns rise in my life. You bring the sparkle of a thousand moons to my soul. Claiming you has brought me such joy that I can't fathom a moment without you," he told me. And then his brow furrowed. "And how do you feel right now?"

I giggled. *Touche.* "I am content. I admit, at first it upset me. I wanted to go back to Earth and forget this vacation. Why doesn't Supernova Escapes just be honest with the humans? It might surprise them at how some would jump at the chance to meet an alien," I said.

"I think there is fear amongst us aliens," he said as

he laughed. "It is a fear that you humans won't go for it. Supernova agents believe the best way for humans to accept their fated mates is to have it happen more naturally. They believe the genetic profile doesn't lie, and eventually the human female will fall madly in love with her alien counterpart. At least, that's the hope. And it seems Supernova Escapes has an impressive record with satisfaction," he chuckled.

"What if I didn't want this? Would you have taken me back to Earth or claimed me against my will?" I held my breath.

"As much as I wanted to claim you the first night I met you, they warned us not to do anything against your will. Humans are very independent beings, having fought to be free for centuries. We were told to respect the process and to let it be mutual," he replied.

"What if I didn't, though? What would you have done?"

Chapter 14

Raven needed reassurances that I wouldn't have claimed her against her will. "I would have taken you back to Earth," I told her. I hoped that would have been the case. We'll never know, because I finally claimed her with her permission. In fact, my body ached to claim her all over again. Alas, duty called.

"Oh, don't leave me," Raven said, her beautiful lips forming a pout.

"My love, we are heading to Salzoni. Unless you want me to take you back to Earth?" I posed the question almost playfully, but had no intention of doing so. My hearts paused as she took more than a moment to think about the question. Her precious face stretched into a brilliant smile.

"I would like nothing more than to see where you are from," she said as she hopped up and grabbed her bag.

My body relaxed as I let out a breath. Perfect. "I'm glad to hear it."

"I thought I was going on vacation to a beautiful world. Astavail is a place I never care to see again. What about your world, what's it like? Have you ever been to Earth?"

I chuckled. "Of course I have. You don't think that

I'd be okay being matched to a Terran without meeting one first, do you?"

Her smile disappeared. "Okay for you, but not a privilege for me, I see?"

I gathered her hands into mine. "I'm sorry for that. It was a rude way to meet your new mate, huh?"

She laughed, and I relaxed. "I'm just teasing you. It's okay. I wouldn't have gone for the whole mail order bride thing, especially to an alien," she admitted.

"Really? Are we aliens all that bad?"

"Well, no. Honestly, I never knew one before you. A lot of the Hollywood stars date aliens. Hot ones," she said while giggling.

"*Hot?*"

She laughed and shook her head. "I forget that some words may not translate well. Hot means you are buff. Sexy. Desirable?"

"Oh! I'll agree then."

My beautiful mate followed me to the bridge. The crew dispersed in my wake, but I stiffened my spine and smiled instead of barking an order.

"Good day," I said to them.

"Yes, yes. It is." Little Avane nodded, looking perplexed as he scurried away. I confused the little crewmember. Raven smiled at me and nodded.

Her fingers slid through mine as we entered the bridge. Bruns' brow shot up as he noticed. "I see that you two had a good rest."

Raven blushed and giggled. "Who rested?" I answered, causing her face to turn a deeper red.

"Well then, congratulations are in order. Looks like

Supernova Escapes scored another perfect match," he replied with a smile.

"Eh, he'll do," Raven said as she perched on the seat to my left. I side-eyed her and smiled as I shook my head. I understood the terminology as it was meant in a joking way. Terrans seemed to joke a lot. I needed to learn to say light-hearted things to her as well.

The ship took off into hyper-speed and approached WormHole J-89. "You're in for a fun trip now. This wormhole will bring us within hours of Salzoni. Before we discovered it, the trip would have taken over two months in hyper-speed," I informed my mate.

Raven whistled. "Okay, I'm belted in," she replied. Her hands squeezed the armrests as we approached and burned through the wormhole, putting us on the fringe of the Humbaba System. The brightly colored planets shone at us with the background nebula, visible only from the outskirts of the system.

"Oh, so beautiful. So colorful. I mean, my system is breathtaking, but nothing like this," Raven told me.

"Wait until you see Salzoni. It's lovely with mountains that reach high into the violet sky, and deep indigo seas frame the lands. Our skies are a violet blue color at the middle of the day. First morning light brings a slight green. It's an oddity, because we're so close to the gaseous planet M'xoh. It rises in the sky along with our three minor moons, all of which are satellite stations to Salzoni. They position our military on one and the other two are places to store ships such as this," I said.

"Does that mean that we won't take the *Remis* down

to Salzoni?"

"Oh no, not at all. We'll take the Sal-Star flight transports."

"It's best since the hull can't take another atmospheric burn until it receives the proper restorations. The nanobots only gave it a bandage to get back home," Bruns said.

"Interesting." Raven turned and looked out over the system as we entered the outer realm, passing through the asteroid belt. Thankfully, the trench zone floated around Humbada on the other side of the system, so we only needed to worry about dodging smaller bits of debris.

Salzoni came into view, and Bruns took great care in explaining every detail of the globe. Raven nodded thoughtfully at his prattle while I worried that she wouldn't like it there.

"Sali Moon 3 welcomes the *Remis*," came the voice over the radio. I smiled as I picked up the comm.

"Hamphh. Good to hear a friendly voice. We fly in with some injuries. Five of us need medical attention. We lost one on Astavail. We also have a special guest. A female Terran, directly from Earth," I told him.

Raven beamed at me as we approached Sali Moon 3.

"She will be quarantined here for a complete day and tested," Hamphh replied.

"Don't worry, it's just a precaution. We need to know the virus won't affect you as it took out nearly all the Salzonian females years ago. If you are not immune, we'll just go elsewhere," I told her.

"Do you think I could be? Are there any other Terrans

on Salzoni?"

I thought for a moment. "I really don't know. There are other female beings. No doubt Supernova Escapes had a role in procuring for our desperate male population." I grinned as I reached for her hand.

"Gotcha. Okay, I'm ready. I hope I'm immune to the virus. I'd love to see your home planet," she answered.

The *Remis* glided into the bay, and once the great doors closed and acclimated, we opened the hatch. Immediately, the medics came to fetch our injured. A Salzonian female approached wearing a medic jacket.

"Where's the Terran?" she asked as she adjusted her face mask.

"Right here," I said as I helped Raven step through the hatch.

While Raven disappeared with the medic, I spoke with the head of maintenance and explained our predicament. Waiting for Raven gave me time to see about my home on the surface. By the end of the waiting period I spoke to the maintenance head again. "I'd like to take my new mate for a ride around the Humbaba System as soon as the ship is ready."

"About a month to add the new hull," he told me.

"That is if I can take my mate to Salzoni first."

"And that will be fine. She's immune to the virus," the medic said as she led Raven to me.

"Wonderful." I took her hand and smiled. "I am so excited to show you my home."

"I'm excited to see it." Raven beamed with the new assurance of excellent health.

Raven and I took a seat on the flight transport, with

her sitting by the window. It took another couple of hours to approach Salzoni since the transports weren't able to reach hyper-speed. Her eyes scanned the horizon as she sucked in a breath. Humbaba rose over the edge, followed by M'Xoh in its radiant glory.

"That has to be the most incredible sight I've ever seen," Raven breathed.

Seeing my planet through Raven's eyes made me appreciate the beauty of it even more. We walked along the village, peppered with businesses and homes along the way.

"You know, I'm a little shocked by all this," she said as she looked around.

"How so?"

"I thought somehow this place would be all much more advanced. I mean, the *Remis* and those moons." Her hand swept upwards as Sali Moon 2 rose in the sky.

"We have some space age industry and have for a long time. Long ago, my people decreed Salzoni remain a natural planet. All heavy industries are on the moons. It keeps our environment clean. Your people could learn this valuable lesson by using the non-atmospheric planets and moons for their industry instead of having it clutter and pollute the Earth," I told her.

Raven grimaced. "Yeah, it took us a long time to enter the space age. I mean, it happened decades before I was born. Before it did, we thought of aliens as legends. Until those reached out to us to help us save our planet. We're harnessing the power of the moon now, as well as Mars. The other planets are more resorts. We have a long way to go," she told me.

The concern dug at my hearts. I had a burning question. I smiled as I took her hand and led her to the outskirts of my tiny village. The land stretched before us and in a valley between two small hills, my small home sat. Hoping to find my mate, I bought it before I left Salzoni months earlier. The rounded roof came into view and Raven squealed.

"Oh, that's the cutest place," she said.

"Do you like it?"

"Yes, I suppose. I'm not sure what it is exactly," she replied.

I pulled around until we reached it. "This is my home," I said as I grinned.

Raven's eyes grew large as she exited the personal transport. Once inside, her hands ran over the furniture, which didn't look too unlike the pieces of furniture found on Earth. "I love it! It reminds me of hobbit homes," she said.

"*Hobbit* homes?"

"Oh, it's a fictional story. Hobbits lived in rounded homes. Nevermind," Raven said as she moved through the rooms. "Strange, so strange. It's all so surreal." She perched on the bed and peered out the window nearby. The majestic indigo mountains loomed high in the distance.

I sat beside her and my hearts pounded as I took her hand. "Raven, I need to know, are you willing?" I searched her eyes.

She turned to me. "Willing?"

"Willing to make Salzoni your home. Willing to help replenish the population?"

"You mean have a baby with you?"

I laughed. "That's the whole point in claiming a mate, to create a family," I replied.

Her brow furrowed. "Not to have me with you. You only want me for my fertility?"

"It's a package deal. If you can never have children with me, I'll be the happiest Salzonian alive with you by my side for the rest of our lives," I said. And I meant it.

Her hand came up and cupped my face. "I would love to have babies with you," she said sweetly. Her eyes stayed on mine as she undressed. "How about we start trying right now?"

Epilogue

RAVEN

Never in a million years did I think my paradise vacation on another planet would turn into a new life. For a year I've lived on Salzoni, a planet many tens of thousands of light-years from Earth in the Humbaba System. Our wedding took place on the *Remis*. At least, that's how Salzonians do it. They mate for life, no exceptions. At first, I thought of Orxlon as a savage asshole. But it didn't take long for me to realize that Supernova Escapes was right and the genetic profile match was perfect.

I am completely and totally in love with my alien husband. The big bronzed brute with his intricately-designed chest intrigues me daily. I wake up each morning with the beautiful colorful sunrise over the indigo mountains. M'xoh rising in the sky never gets old. Orxlon says it's a gas planet. We can't land there as it's much like Saturn in my home system. I don't mind.

What would my parents think? I often think about this and miss them terribly. But they perished doing something that they loved, traveling through space. When we celebrated our six months on Salzoni, Orxlon took me for a spin through the Humbaba System. It took three weeks as we snuck in and out of hyper-speed to each of the fifteen planets. Most had habitations of different beings, some planets being tropical and others being frozen and locked in a perpetual winter. The wonders of this system never cease to amaze me.

This morning I have a surprise for my alien husband. The life inside my belly quickens, much sooner than I expected. Dr. Osh assures me all is well.

Orxlon beams as he gently lifts me, and we twirl. "Really?" His eyes scan the report from Dr. Osh.

Uncertainty happens even in the best of times. My belly grows too quickly, and it scares me. My mind flits to the old alien movies, before Earth had contact with the real thing. But Orxlon is very human like, and our genetics are so closely aligned.

SEVEN MONTHS LATER

Lying in the medical facility, the doctor hands us our girls. *Twin girls!* They are beautiful and look very much like me, except for their golden eyes, and the smaller intricate design on their little torsos.

"They are perfect. No sign that they carry the illness that befalls Salzonian females," Dr. Osh says.

I snuggle into my mate's side as we hold our newborn daughters. The future looks bright with the promise of better tomorrows for the Salzonian race.

About the Authors

Eden Ember

Eden Ember found her passion in writing sci-fi romance. She spends her days either pounding on the keyboard or dreaming up the next stories. Her active imagination never lets up and the perfect outlet comes through in her books.

Join Eden Ember's exclusive reader's list
- New Books, Hot Sales, and Freebies
- Eden's reader giveaways
- EXCLUSIVE sneak peeks at upcoming novels
- First look at Covers
- Who Eden Recommends (Love me some SCI FI Romance!)

EdenEmber.com

Starr Huntress

Starr Huntress is a coalition of the brightest Starrs in romance banding together to explore uncharted territories.

If you like your men horny- maybe literally- and you're equal opportunity skin color- because who doesn't love a guy with blue or green skin?- then join us as we dive into swashbuckling space adventure, timeless romance, and lush alien landscapes.

Sign up for the newsletter for giveaways, promotions and new release announcements: http://eepurl.com/b_NJyr

www.ingramcontent.com/pod-product-compliance
Lightning Source LLC
Chambersburg PA
CBHW031437150726
47989CB00002B/966